From Granny
To Forbes.

Xmas 192[...]

20p -
Red Cross

D0707989

THE NECKLACE OF SHELLS

HE ALLOWED THEM TO EXAMINE AT THEIR LEISURE THE
SHELL NECKLACE THAT HE WORE.

THE
NECKLACE OF SHELLS
A STORY OF WEST AFRICA

BY

DAVID KER

ILLUSTRATED BY

J. R. BURGESS

LONDON
"THE BOY'S OWN PAPER" OFFICE
4 BOUVERIE STREET, E.C.4

Made in Great Britain
Printed by the Religious Tract Society
4 Bouverie Street, E.C.4

CONTENTS

CHAP.   PAGE

I. A Mysterious Boy 9

II. At Close Quarters with Death . 27

III. The Black Crew 39

IV. Vanished in the Night . . . 55

V. A Startling Apparition . . . 72

VI. Bad News 92

VII. An Unseen Enemy 102

VIII. The Coming of the Destroyers . 121

IX. Prisoners 134

X. To Live or Die ? 149

XI. Doomed 166

XII. The Last Sunrise 182

ILLUSTRATIONS

HE ALLOWED THEM TO EXAMINE AT THEIR
LEISURE THE SHELL NECKLACE THAT HE
WORE . . . . *Coloured frontispiece*

PAGE

UP ROSE THE SNAKE'S HEAD WITH A SHARP
ANGRY HISS 41

" JENOR-FLAN, AND NO MISTAKE ! " . . 169

THE
NECKLACE OF SHELLS

CHAPTER I

A MYSTERIOUS BOY

" I WONDER who he can be ; he looked just like a prince, and he spoke like one, too."

" Well, very likely he may have been a prince in his own country. You remember Stanley's ' Kalulu '—a real ' Black Prince,' sure enough."

" I'd give something to know all about that shell necklace that he wore. It has a history of its own, I'll be bound."

" And a pretty queer one too, I dare say ; he told us, you know, that it was a ' ju-ju ' " (magic charm).

So spoke the two English lads who were standing on the brow of the great ridge that overhangs Funchal, the capital of

the invalid, leaning for rest on his staff,
" and I must do like most hill-climbers
when they are tired and don't want to
show it—halt and admire the view."

The view, in fact, well deserved the
admiration that it has received in all ages,
since brave Commodore Zargo first looked
upon it in 1419.

True, time has robbed the charming
little island of some of its most picturesque
features and most ancient monuments.
The noble forests that gave it the name
of Madeira (wood) have been swept away
along the whole southern side of the island,
and we may now look in vain for the
abundant growth of fennel (funcho) whence
the capital was named Funchal. The old
Franciscan convent at the western gate
is represented only by a few heaps of
crumbling stone, and modern civilization
has demolished the fine old house of Jean
d'Esmenaut in the Rua do Esmeraldo to
make room for a co-operative store.

But nothing can mar the splendour of the towering hills cleft by steep black gorges, the glittering waterfalls bounding from ledge to ledge of the lava rocks, the deep-green patches of corn or flax on the lower slopes, the brighter tint of the plumy sugar-cane, the white-fronted *quintas* (villas) far up the hillside, peeping shyly through the dark, glossy foliage of embowering gardens or orchards, the frowning precipices, the shadowy pine-woods hanging like clouds along the highest ridges, the grim ruins of ancient forts standing gauntly up against the sky, the wide blue sea with its foaming breakers, and the endless windings of the cliffs, chequered with every gradation of colour, from the pale yellow of the crumbling sandstone to the cindery blackness of the volcanic lava.

" By-the-bye," said Dr Strong suddenly, "what were you young men talking of so earnestly when I came up ? "

" Oh, we've had quite an adventure,"

said Dick. " Coming down that hill over there we met a black boy who was limping badly, so we hailed him, to know if we could do him any good ; and we found he had a regular sore on his left foot, poor chap, that must have hurt like anything. Luckily I had that ointment of yours in my pocket, in case old Ric here should be footsore ; so I tore a bit off that old cloth that held our sandwiches, and put some of the stuff on it, and tied up his foot for him."

" And then," put in Eric, " he thanked us as if he were some king or other ; and seeing that he looked hungry, we gave him all that was left of the sandwiches, and he seemed jolly glad to get 'em ! "

" And what do you think ? " cried Dick, " he had heard of my father, and thought he must have seen him once, over there ; and he said that in his country the people call Daddy ' the good white man.' "

" It is a sad thing to think of," said Strong gravely, " that all African savages represent the Evil One himself in the form of a *white* man—just shows what sort of white men they have had to deal with. Well, what happened next ? "

" Well, of course we wanted him to stay and tell us all about it ; but he said he couldn't stop, for he had to take a message to his master, Dom Pablo (Paul) da Silva."

" Da Silva ! " echoed the doctor, " the very man I am going to see to-night about a house of his that I think may suit me, between Santa Cruz and Machico."

" Well, then, uncle," cried Eric, " do find out, if you can, who that black boy is. I *do* want to know all about him—I'm sure he's a prince ! "

" And if you get a chance," added Dick, " please ask about that shell necklace that he wears ; he says it's a kind of magic charm."

But their curiosity on both points had to remain unsatisfied for the present ; for when the doctor came back from his call that evening, he met their eager inquiries with a shake of the head.

" I have nothing to tell you about your black prince, my boys," said he ; " in fact, I got no chance to ask about him. You see, a man like Dom Pablo, a real Portuguese *fidalgo*[1] of the old school, is not the sort of person with whom you can talk very freely at your first meeting ; you have to stand a good deal on ceremony, and ask no questions. He's rather a forbidding fellow, too, and I fancy your black friend can't have a very pleasant life of it with him."

The boys looked blank ; but Strong went on without seeming to notice it.

" Now, I'll tell you what I've arranged. We'll go over to Santa Cruz to-morrow, and put up at the hotel ; and then, if the house suits us, we'll just move in at once. I'm sending off our luggage by bullock-cart,

[1] " Filho d' algo " (literally " son of some one ") the term for a man of rank. The Spanish form is *hidalgo*.

and I'm going in a hammock myself ; but I suppose you two would sooner walk."

"Oh, rather!" cried Dick, "it will be just like exploring a new country, and twelve miles won't hurt us, eh, Ric ? "

Next morning, just after breakfast, away went Dr Strong in his hammock—the hammock being in Madeira what the cab is in England—between two men whose long, swinging stride combined the maximum of speed with the minimum of shaking, and was just the thing for an invalid. Having seen him off, and made their own preparations, the two lads tramped off in turn at their best speed.

Away, away, in the bright morning sunshine, along the endless windings of the cliff-road, between the white waves that dashed and roared a hundred feet below, and the purple mountains that towered against the clear blue sky two thousand feet above. Is there anything to beat a brisk walk, in fine weather, through a

B

perfectly new country ?   Dick thought not, and said so, and his chum quite agreed with him.

In truth, there was plenty to see.   Now they were looking down over a low wall into a golden sea of feathery sugar-canes, swaying drowsily to and fro in the fresh morning breeze.   The next moment they were overshadowed by a huge, dark cliff, from one of the clefts of which a dwarfish, goblin-like form clad in filthy tatters extended a misshapen hand with a whining petition for alms.

A shout made them spring aside just in time to avoid the lop-sided rush of an ox-drawn sled laden with faggots, and steered with a short cord by a sun-browned peasant from the hills, whose matted hair was surmounted with a queer little black skull-cap with a long spike sticking up from the top of it, very much like an umbrella blown inside out.   Then the scene changed once more, and they were hanging in mid-air above a deep, dark, narrow gorge, from the rocky sides of which the spiky bosses of the prickly pear thrust themselves out in every direction, while through its depths a foaming torrent, swollen by the melting of the mountain snows, roared downward to the sea.

" I wonder if we shall meet our ' Black Prince ' on the way," said Eric as they tramped along.

" I dare say we shall," cried Dick, " and if we do, we'll find out something about him this time, if we have to hold him upside down and turn him inside out."

As he spoke, the road seemed to run headlong down into the middle of a quiet little village tucked away in a snug hollow. The whole of the steep descent was paved with smooth, round cobble-stones, as slippery as glass ; and Dick was just warning his chum to mind and not get a tumble, when he suddenly got one himself. His foot slipped, and he went sprawling on his back in the middle of the road, amid a roar of laughter from the dozen or so of villagers who watched his fall from the doors of their huts.

But Dick was not so silly as to get angry at his mishap. Up he jumped, and joined in the laugh as heartily as anyone —to the visible approval of the sturdy peasants, who hastily dusted him down, and sent after him a hearty "Boa viagem, Senhor!" (good journey, sir) as he went striding up the hill beyond, with Eric at his heels.

Just at the top of it they passed to the right, on a projecting bluff overhanging the sea, a gloomy pile of grey, moss-grown masonry, massive even in ruin, in the shattered front of which three or four crumbling loop-holes still bore silent witness of that grim age when every man's hand was against his neighbour. But now a tumble-down hut had been pieced together in one corner of it, and half a dozen pigs filled the mouldering walls with sounds widely different from those which awoke their echoes in the days of long ago.

" What a shame ! " cried Eric indignantly, " to turn that fine old ruin into a pig-sty ! "

" Well, I don't know ; the fellows who lived there in old times must have been such awful pigs that, after all, it's only keeping it in the family."

Just then they were startled by a squeaking and squealing like the death cries of a thousand pigs at once, a music due to the ungreased wheels of a bullock-carriage, a kind of hearse on wheels drawn by two stout oxen, which were guided, as the boys found to their amusement, by reins made fast to the tips of their horns !

On, on, with unflagging speed, till they crowned the ridge above Porto Novo, from whence they could see the tiny fishing hamlet lying right in the pebbly river-bed, as if, said Eric, it had just been washed down from the hills by a freshet !

The light faded from tree-top after tree-top till the pine-woods in their turn were shrouded in ghostly shadow; and, last of all, the vast castellated precipices above faded sullenly from crimson to grey, and all was gloom.

"Push along, old boy!" cried Dick, forcing a laugh; "they say we're growing pretty fast, so we don't need watering!"

But, joke as he might, Dick was inwardly in no jesting mood. The whole sky was now black as night, and as he looked up at it a pale gleam of lightning quivered along the dim horizon, and from the far distance came a low growl of thunder.

By this time the road was quite deserted; for the native peasants needed no one to tell them what was coming, and had fled to shelter long before. Onward over an endless zigzag of break-neck ascents and descents, the whole country being cut up by a succession of gullies and water-courses; and at every new turn of the way Dick

looked eagerly out for Santa Cruz.   But he
looked in vain ; and, worse still, his chum—
less seasoned than himself to hard exercise
—was visibly beginning to flag.

With the storm just about to burst on
them, and his comrade's strength failing,
poor Dick was almost tempted to give it up
as a bad job, and take refuge in one of the
caves that honeycombed the cliffs around
him, wet and dark as they were. He was
just turning to propose this to Eric, when
a sharp bend of the road revealed Santa
Cruz itself just before them, with its trim
white houses nestling around the meek
little grey church, in front of which, amid
a group of beautiful til-trees, stood the
slender crucifix of marble that has now
replaced the rough wooden cross whence
the village took its name ; and to the left,
just beyond a small sugar plantation, lay
the hotel whither they were bound !

The boys hailed it with a cheer ; but just
then fell sullenly on their upturned faces,

early bathe—not venturing far out, however, for fear of sharks—and had swum about among the wave-lashed rocks and weed-clad reefs, till Dick, thrown by a wave on to a limpet ledge, was scraped to and fro against it by the tide till he was, in his own phrase, " as sore as if he had had two dozen with a cat-o'-nine-tails." Better still, they had made a full inspection of the far-famed Machico Valley, which lay only three or four miles farther up the coast.

Hidden, like all the other sea-board villages of Madeira, in a deep gully between two hills, Machico came upon them, when they first saw it, as a kind of surprise. The road thither along the brow of the cliff, with the mountains above and the sea below, was even more picturesque than that from Funchal to Santa Cruz ; but the crowning glory of the grand panorama was certainly the Valley of Machico itself.

Acres of green corn patches and golden fields of sugar-cane, dotted here and there with the dark, glossy foliage of terraced gardens, sloped downward beneath the mighty shadow of the grim precipices that towered more than a thousand feet over-head.   From the great height at which the boys stood, the tiny bay, over which a few brightly painted boats were flitting like fireflies, looked smooth as a mirror between the vast black cliffs that walled it in ; and only by the ring of foam that girdled the shingly beach, and the dull growl of the champing pebbles ground against each other by the back-wash of the surf, could they tell that beneath that calm, bright surface heaved the unresting swell of the Atlantic.

Among the clustering trees out of which the square white tower of the village church peered like an ambushed sentinel, they could dimly see the dark gateway and grey, crumbling wall of one of the countless forts that studded this coast in days when the whole sea around it bristled with Moorish

corsairs; and, on a rock ledge overhanging
the chafing breakers, they found a tiny
chapel of stone, marking the spot where the
ill-fated pair from whom Machico takes its
name lie buried in one grave.

As yet the boys had heard only a few
vague hints of that simple, touching story;
and at their eager request Dr Strong told
it to them in full, that same evening, in
words of fire.

In the spring of 1419 João Gonsalvez
Zargo, the Captain Cook of Portugal, came
into port with a sallow, weather-beaten
Spanish castaway on board, whom he had
picked up off the coast of Andalusia.   Prince
Henry the Navigator, ever on the watch for
fresh news from the sea that he loved, sent
for the Spaniard, who told a strange and
stirring tale.

He had been the pilot of a Bristol barque,
hired by a young Englishman of noble
blood, Robert Machim by name, who was
flying from home with his secretly wedded

bride, Anna D'Arfet, to escape the venge-
ance of her hostile kinsmen.   But a furious
northerly gale drove them far out of
their course, and stranded them at last
on an uninhabited and hitherto unknown
island !

One can fancy how the Prince's eyes
sparkled at those words, and how eagerly he
listened as Juan Morales went on to describe
the noble mountains of the mysterious land,
its sunny skies, its ever-flowing streams, its
shadowy forests, its sheltered bays and
towering cliffs, and all the grand features of
that wonderful panorama which, marvellous
even to the prosaic eye of the twentieth
century, seemed a perfect fairyland when
seen through the heated fancy and high-
flown description of a superstitious mariner
of the fifteenth.

"But, in good truth, your highness," went
on the old seaman, with a slight tremor in
his gruff voice, "it seemed as if God Himself fought against us, for, ere we could land

our stores or make provision in any wise for our dwelling ashore, lo! the tempest that had driven us thither arose again and drave our ship from her moorings into the open sea, that she was seen no more. The which ill-chance was so grievous to the fair Lady Anna (she being weak from long watching and much sorrow) that right suddenly she gave up her soul to God, holding in her hands the hands of the young lord from England, and looking up in his face even unto the end—a right pitiful sight, in truth, as ever mine eyes looked on. Then he, as not willing to be left alone, in a few days thereafter died likewise, praying us with his last breath to lay him in one tomb with his bride, and, if ever God should grant us to see our homes again, to return and build a Christian church over their grave."

In the course of their rambles among the hills the boys had again met, once or twice, the mysterious negro lad whom they called

" The Black Prince," herding a number of goats as black and wild-looking as himself. But though they did their best to find out all about him, he seemed strangely shy of answering any questions, and, in fact, said as little as he well could; and they began to suspect that Dr Strong had rightly guessed that he had no very happy life of it with his present master, Dom Pablo da Silva.

He allowed them, however, to examine at their leisure the shell necklace that he wore, a very picturesque specimen of savage adornment. The shells, which were strung on a cord of twisted palm fibre, were tinted with red at the edges, every fifth shell being larger than the rest, and the clasp that fastened the chain was a leopard's claw!

When they asked eagerly who had killed the leopard, he replied simply that he had slain it himself; an admission which, made by a boy hardly as old as themselves, sounded quite heroic to them both. In

c

fact, their account of this marvel so much impressed the doctor that he was bent on seeing it for himself, and bade the boys ask their black friend to come to the house the first time he passed near it on his way home.

But this was easier said than done, for during the next few days the Black Prince was nowhere to be seen, though they went again and again to the spot where they had met him before.

" Well, I'll tell you what, old boy," cried Fernott, "we'll go up to-morrow and have one more try to find him, and if we can't, we must just get Uncle George to write and ask Dom Pablo to send him over to us, necklace and all."

" Right you are ! " said Wyse, and the very next morning they turned their backs on the shore and plunged into the silence of the lonely hills.

The first mile or so was no joke, thanks to the slippery cobble-stones that paved the break-neck path, giving them the feeling of

climbing up the side of a house coated
with greased nuts.   But without this breast-
plate the light soil would be swept down in
cart-loads by the first shower, as they began
to see when they got higher up and found
the "road" degenerating into a mere
torrent-bed, hacked into holes two or three
feet deep.

One by one the tiny cottages, looking like
stamps pasted on the hill-side, were left
behind.   Barking dogs and begging children
tailed off together.   The poor little patches
of vegetation, planted by the struggling
peasants on every ledge of the cliffs,
gradually disappeared.   The close, heavy
air grew fresh, breezy, bracing, and the
boys drank it in with eager delight.

"When I'm old enough," cried Dick
warmly, "I'll go and explore some new
country, see if I don't!   Mustn't it be fine
to go where no one has ever been before!
I'd rather have been Columbus than any
man I know."

" And *he* lived here once, by the by," said Eric; "you remember Uncle George telling us how the people thought him mad, and wondered why he was always poring over those maps and charts of his.   Hullo ! "

He might well cry " hullo," for at that moment the ground to right and left seemed to fall away all at once, and they were picking their way along a knife-edge of rock just wide enough for one at a time !

Happily both lads were steady of foot and head, for one slip would have sent them bumping down from ledge to ledge for more than five hundred feet, to plunge at last into the waterfall whose dull roar hardly reached their ears, or to spike themselves on a pine which, though it looked a mere twig from that tremendous height, was really tall enough for the mast of a merchant barque. But the perilous isthmus was soon past, and the gloom and silence of the pine-woods that clad the mountain-top closed round them like a shroud.

Suddenly, however, in the depth of the ghostly forest, they came upon a small grassy clearing on which the sun was now shining with its full power.

The turf looked very inviting after their long uphill struggle, and soon they were seated on it side by side, leaning their backs snugly against a moss-grown rock; nor was it long ere Wyse, tired with his long climb and drowsy from the heat, dozed off to sleep.

Not so the ever-restless Dick, who was too brim-full of life to keep still for five minutes. He soon grew tired of doing nothing, and jumped up with the intention of going deeper into the wood and trying to find the mysterious lad whom they were seeking.

" Old Ric can't come to any harm while I'm away," said he, looking back at his sleeping chum; "it's not as if there were any wild beasts about, and I won't be gone five minutes."

Little did he guess what was to happen in that five minutes' absence!

He had not gone far when the tinkle of a small bell was heard and out of the rustling, crackling thicket came three or four black goats.

" Here are our black friend's goats, so he can't be far off," muttered our hero. " Ten to one he's found Ric and is having a yarn with him ; I'll go back and see."

He was soon back in the clearing, but hardly had he entered it when he caught sight of something that stopped him short as if turned to stone.

Eric was still sleeping quietly, but what was that glittering object that lay on his breast ? At first it looked not unlike a flat metal plate ; but a second glance showed Dick, to his unspeakable horror, the glistening scales and flat narrow head of a deadly snake !

CHAPTER III

THE BLACK CREW

COOL and brave as Dick Fernott was, this sight of horror came upon him so suddenly that he quite lost his head for a moment, and stood gazing helplessly, not knowing what to do.

What *could* he do, in fact? The snake lay quite still, coiled up as if asleep; but at any moment the sleeping boy might make some movement that would provoke the reptile to plunge its deadly fangs into his flesh. On the other hand, Dick could not strike at it without wounding Eric himself; and, in any case, unless he could be sure of killing it at the first blow, it would still have life enough left to deal the boy his death stroke before it died.

What was to be done? Milk, he had read, has a great attraction for snakes; but

there was none at hand. For an instant
he thought of tossing the serpent off Eric's
chest with a forked stick; but, curled up
as it was, this would be no easy matter,
and certain death to his friend if he failed.

Poor Dick was quite at a loss how to
act, yet act he must, and that quickly ;
for at any instant Eric might awake and
move, and all would then be over.

But just then a dark form came gliding
toward him from among the trees, which
he knew at a glance, to his intense relief,
as their " Black Prince."

Dick held up one hand in warning
while pointing to the snake with the other ;
but it was needless, for the black's keen
eye had already taken in the whole situation. Quick as thought he snatched a
stick from the ground and began to tickle
gently, with its point, the serpent's outer-
most coil, while Dick, white as a sheet,
held his breath to watch the result.

Up rose the snake's head with a sharp,

UP ROSE THE SNAKE'S HEAD WITH A SHARP ANGRY HISS

angry hiss, and it leaped right off Eric's chest toward its disturber.

"Thank God!" said Dick fervently, "old Ric is safe!"

His heart beat quick, however, as he saw the horrible creature dart at the rescuer; but, quick as it was, the negro was quicker still. Springing nimbly aside, he struck it a sharp blow across the neck with his stick, stunning it for a moment, and instantly one stamp of his bare heel crushed the flat head into the earth, killing the snake on the spot.

Dick's lusty hurrah would have broken a sounder sleep than Eric's, and the latter started up and stared around him in bewilderment. But he could easily guess the whole story from the sight of the dead snake and the radiant face of his chum, who, seizing the conqueror's hand in both his own, cried, "Well done, Prince! you're a hero!"

"How you know me prince? me no tell

you," said the other in broken Portuguese, with a keen glance at him.

Dick, to whose lips the familiar nickname had come quite naturally, without any afterthought, started slightly at this sudden confirmation of their strange guess.

" It was easy to see that," he replied. " But what is your real name at home ? "

" Jenor-Flan," said the negro lad proudly. " Prince Jenor-Flan, man call me in my country."

Eric, who had listened to all this with marked interest, now came forward in turn to offer his thanks to his rescuer, who seemed to think very little of the feat himself, now that it was done.

" You been good to me," said he simply ; " me glad do what can for you."

Then Dick told the prince that they had come out on purpose to find him and ask him to come to their cottage the next time he passed ; for their guardian, the Senhor Strong, had heard of his magic necklace, and wished much to see it, he being himself a " fetish man " of great renown.

This seemed to Dick the best mode of conveying to an African savage the idea of a man of science; and, in fact, Jenor-Flan's face assumed, at the last words, a look of visible interest.

" White man know fetish too ? " asked he in a tone of surprise.

" To be sure he does ! " cried Dick; " he can do all sorts of wonders. I dare say he'll show you a few when you come."

The black's eyes sparkled, and he at once agreed to come that evening to their cottage, which he must pass on his way home; and then they parted, the two chums going down the hill again, while Jenor-Flan went to see after his goats.

But the excitements of that eventful morning were not ended yet. As the boys turned to go down the slope Eric suddenly saw, or thought he saw, a *face* amid the clustering leaves of the nearest thicket—

a grim, savage, pitch-black face, with its eyes fixed hungrily on Jenor-Flan's receding form in a look of fierce joy such as might be worn by a tigress which, having vainly sought her missing cub through the whole jungle, should all at once espy it lying unhurt within easy reach of her.

Just for one moment that goblin visage stood plain to view, and then it was gone as if it had never been.

"Look! look!" cried Eric excitedly, as he pointed to the spot.

"What's up?" cried the wondering Dick. "What did you see?"

"A face among those bushes that looked very wickedly at Jenor-Flan."

"A face in there?" laughed Dick. "My dear fellow, no man on earth could get through that thicket without making a row like fifty sticks of sealing-wax all breaking at once, and I haven't heard a sound. It must have been only your fancy, take my word for it."

" Well, I certainly thought I saw it," said Eric, looking puzzled.

" That's just it, you thought you did. Now take my advice and think you didn't."

And then no more was said about it— for the time.

When they got home Dr Strong heard, with no small interest, the tale of Eric's danger and Jenor-Flan's daring, and warmly declared that he must find some way to reward the boy prince's courage as it deserved.

" Well, I'll tell you what you might do, uncle," cried Dick. " You say yourself he don't seem very happy with old Dom Pablo, so why shouldn't you buy him (I dare say the old Dom would let him go cheap) and take him to England with us, or send him home to his own country, whichever he liked best."

" Not at all a bad idea, my boy; I'll think it over.   What now, Eric?   You look as if you wanted to say something."

Eric, still persuaded that he had really seen the goblin face in the thicket, told all about it in a few words.

"Well," cried Strong, "if he has an enemy among the blacks here, that is all the more reason to get him out of harm's way. I'll have a talk with him when he comes, and see Dom Pablo about it to-morrow."

Dr Strong kept his word, and when he and Jenor-Flan came out of the doctor's study (in which the promised talk had been held) the boys, who were waiting eagerly to see what would come of it, noticed that while the boy prince's face was radiant with joy, Strong himself looked very grave and a good deal perplexed.

"Then you agree," they heard him say to Jenor-Flan, "to lend me your necklace. I won't do it any harm, you know; I just want to make a drawing of it."

"One night you have him, no keep him more!" said the black prince, with a look and tone so commanding that as Eric (who was fond of history) afterwards said, it just reminded him of "old Noll Cromwell breaking up the Long Parliament."

Off went Jenor-Flan without a word more, and the doctor set to work on his drawing of the famous chain. But all at once he stopped short, and, looking at his watch, said hastily :

" I think I'll just go and see Da Silva at once about this job, and get it over. It's early yet, and this is just the time to find him over his after-dinner cigar, when he is sure to be in a good humour."

" If he is ever in one at all ! " muttered Dick, with whom Dom Pablo was no favourite.

" I dare say I shall be away some time, though," went on Strong; " so what will you young men do till I come back ? "

At that very moment, as if in reply to his query, a voice said under the verandah on which they sat :

" Do the Senhores care for a sail to-night ?
It is a fine evening."

Both lads knew the voice of Joam (John)
Lopez, an old native boatman with whom
they had often gone on the water before,
and Dick called out eagerly :

" Just the very thing ! You'll come too,
won't you, Uncle George ? we can wait
till you get back, easy enough."

" No, you had better not wait, for I
don't suppose I shall be home much before
supper. Off you go, and good luck to you."

That cruise was one which the boys were
long to remember.

In the glory of the moonlight, which
made every ripple a silvery flash, the wide
expanse of smooth water around them
looked like a fairy sea where storms were
unknown ; and the vast, shadowy mountains that towered above them against the
star-lit sky might well have passed for
some enchanted cloudland of old romance,
to roll away at the first beam of sunrise.

D

The silence and mystery and romance of the whole scene were just to the taste of the boys, and old Lopez (who, though he could neither read nor write, had the romantic history of his native island at his finger-ends, and loved to pour himself out upon it to these lads who listened to him so eagerly) began at once to talk of how brave Commodore Zargo and his daring crew had glided along this very coast ages ago, past headland after headland and precipice after precipice, till they swept at last into a smooth basin flanked by a strip of pebble beach, over which a tiny river ran down into the sea. Right across its course, scores of stately trees, uptorn by a recent whirlwind, lay heaped together like fallen warriors ; and the stout old commodore, reverently doffing his plumed hat, said with that mingling of romance and religion that marked the mediaeval cavalier :

" ' See, my sons ! God hath given us

timber to build Him a temple and plant Him a cross here in the wilderness, where no man hath set foot till now. We will do it forthwith ; and this spot shall henceforth bear the name of Santa Cruz.' "

But the great event of the evening was yet to come.

Doubling a sharp point, they suddenly saw right ahead of them, not a cable's length away, a long, low, rakish-looking brigantine, which, though not anchored, was hove-to as if she had some special business at that particular spot, and, in fact, her men were just lowering a boat as if to go ashore.

The moment Lopez caught sight of her he gave a violent start, and, with a muttered exclamation of terror, " backed " his oars so as to bring the boat at once to a standstill ; and, in truth, the sight before them was weird enough to have impressed a far stronger mind than that of the superstitious old seaman.

Themselves unseen in the deep shadow of the headland, they could make out plainly, in the glorious moonlight, every point of the brigantine, even to the faces of her crew. The vessel herself, and all belonging to her, were as black as night— her masts, the planking of her deck, and her very sails. Moreover, she had a crew to match, clad in black, and with jet-black hands and faces, which, with the sudden gleam of their white teeth in the moonlight, and the rolling of the whites of their great eyes, made them look as grim a set of goblins as Dante himself could have imagined.

The strange vessel showed no lights of any kind, and this fact, coupled with the silent, stealthy putting-off of the boat, which, while they were watching it, glided away behind a projecting cliff and was lost to view, bred in the mind of the shrewd lads a suspicion that Dick was not slow to utter.

"These chaps must be smugglers, and no mistake!" said he in a whisper, "and that, of course, is why they have their sails blackened, so as not to be seen in the dark. It's a queer idea to have a crew all niggers; but perhaps that is to make sure of their not being seen in the dark, too."

"Smugglers, say you, Senhor?" faltered old Lopez in a trembling voice, making the sign of the cross with a hand that quivered like a leaf. "If it were only that I should not mind a bit—I have been a smuggler myself; but these are no smugglers—they are evil spirits! I have heard of such demon-ships many a time, but I never thought to see one with my own eyes. For pity's sake, let us be off at once, or we are all lost!"

The boys did not believe a word of any such nonsense, but they saw plainly that the man was thoroughly frightened, and that to contradict him would only make

him worse; and they wisely judged it
best to give way.

Back they went round the point, undetected by the brigantine's crew, and got
home a good deal later than they had
intended; but, late as they were, they
found that Dr Strong had not yet come
back from the visit on which so much
depended.

CHAPTER IV

VANISHED IN THE NIGHT

THE next morning our three travellers sat over their breakfast (which was wont to be the gayest meal of the day) silent and gloomy, no one speaking a word.

For this, in truth, there was but too good reason, for every one of the three had a special cause of disquiet. Dr Strong was usually the life of the party, but to-day he had plainly some trouble on his mind, and what that trouble was the observant boys were at no loss to guess.

He had come back from his call on Dom Pablo da Silva the night before with so gloomy a face that the boys flew at once to the conclusion that his attempt to purchase Jenor-Flan's freedom had been a failure. Not a word did he say, however, as to what had taken place, and the lads, seeing that he did not wish to talk of it just then, wisely forbore to vex him with indiscreet questions, and waited in no small anxiety till he should think fit to tell them the result himself.

The boys, on their part, were burdened with a secret of their own—the mystery of the suspicious brigantine and her black crew, of which they had said nothing as yet, from a fear of getting old Lopez into trouble ; for they had not forgotten his avowal that he had himself been a smuggler, and took it for granted that he was some-how mixed up with these midnight prowlers. But both lads felt sure (though they could not tell why) that there was more in this strange affair than any mere ordinary smuggling job ; and they were quite as uneasy under the burden of their secret as the doctor under his.

Not a word was spoken till the meal was all but over, and then the first to break the gloomy silence was Dr Strong himself.

" Well, boys, it was kind of you not to bother me with questions last night when you saw I was not in the humour for it, but you will have to know all about this job sooner or later, so I may as well tell you at once that I have done no good."

" What ? won't Dom Pablo part with him, then ? " cried Dick.

" On the contrary, he was quite willing to sell him to me, and to sell him cheap, too ; but he added a condition that upsets the whole business."

" Like the fellow in the story, I suppose," said Dick, forcing a laugh : " ' Did he refuse ? ' ' Not exactly, but he attached a rather burdensome condition.' ' What was it ? ' ' He said he'd see me hanged first ! ' "

The doctor laughed, too, in spite of himself.

" Well, my boy, I'm afraid that *is* very

much what it amounts to, for his condition is that the lad shall give up to him that shell-necklace he wears."

The listening boys eyed him and each other in blank dismay.

"It's all up, then," said Dick ruefully, "for I have heard Jenor-Flan himself say that he wouldn't part with that chain for all the money in Funchal."

"But why does Dom Pablo want the chain so much?" asked Eric; "does he collect curios, then?"

"Well, I really think (though I dare say you can hardly believe that such a thing could be in our day) that Da Silva actually believes it *is* a magic chain, and wants to have it that it may bring him good luck!"

"You don't mean that, Uncle George?" cried both lads at once.

"I do, indeed. You have no idea how these old beliefs cling, and I can tell you that, in some of these out-of-the-way places they have quite as strong a grip of the gentleman as of the peasant. Why, when I was in the east of Russia, I dined with a countess, an educated woman of fashion, who reached right across me rather than let me hand her the salt, which is believed to be unlucky, you know."

" Well, if he really wanted the chain," said Dick, " why didn't he take it from him long ago ? "

" I suppose he thought that if he took it by force, it would bring him bad luck instead of good."

" That's all right, then ! " cried Dick, "let the prince refuse to give it up and the old chap won't dare to take it from him."

" Yes ; but in that case, don't you see, he will be more determined than ever not to part with the lad, for that would be parting with the chain, too. No, unless I can persuade him to think better of it (of which there is not much chance, I fear) poor Jenor-Flan will be as ill off as ever."

At that moment hurried footsteps were heard approaching.

"Here comes Jenor-Flan himself, I expect," said the doctor, "to take back his chain, for he said I was only to keep it one night. Poor lad! I wish I had any good news to give him!"

But he was mistaken. It was a booted heel that rang on the hard ground, and the figure that came hurrying round the corner of the house was that of Dom Pablo da Silva!

"So, Mr Englishman!" cried he, turning upon the startled three a face all aflame with rage, "*this* is how you keep faith with me!"

"I beg your pardon, Senhor——" began Strong, looking puzzled, as in truth he well might.

"Did I not treat you fairly about that lad?" broke in Da Silva fiercely, "and were not the terms I offered you low enough, that you must steal him from me to get him for nothing ? "

The boys flushed up at once at this affront, as if it had been offered to themselves, but Strong only replied quietly but very firmly :

" Steal, Senhor Dom Pablo, is not a word that I can allow any man to apply to me. You call yourself a gentleman and I call myself one, so let us talk, if you please, as two gentlemen ought to do."

It was a favourite boast of the boys that " no one ever dared to give any cheek to Uncle George," and just so it was now.   Dr Strong's cold and dignified composure over-bore at once the childish passion of the angry old man, who, after standing silent for a moment, resumed in a much more subdued tone :

" If I have judged hastily, Senhor, I ask your pardon, but the fact is that the negro lad whom you wished to buy of me is gone,

no one knows where or how, and his magic
chain is gone too ! "

The boys looked meaningly at each other,
but Strong himself, startled as he was by
the astounding news, did not lose his head
for an instant. He knew better than to
say a word of the chain being in his own
possession to a man who was plainly in
no mood to hear reason, and whose un-
just suspicions such an avowal would only
have confirmed, and he replied as calmly
as ever :

" If the noble Senhor will be pleased to
take a seat and tell me all he knows of the
matter, I shall be most happy to give him
all the help in my power. My servants can
assure him that the boy is not here, and the
Senhor is perfectly welcome to search my
house if he thinks fit."

Finding his rudeness met with such
studied courtesy, Da Silva began to feel
ashamed of his violence. Muttering a few
confused words of apology, he took the chair

offered him by Strong and proceeded to tell his story.

Jenor-Flan had come home as usual the night before, and having had his supper, had gone to his sleeping-place—a small hut formerly used as a store-shed, and assigned to him because no place could be found for him in the crowded servants' quarters. No one had seen him since; and as he did not appear with the rest when they were mustered for work next morning, the native overseer had sent a man to fetch him, and his hut was found to be empty!

Dr Strong heard the tale to an end with close attention, but ere he could speak Eric Wyse broke in excitedly :

"The face! the black face in the thicket!"

Strong's brow darkened, for he saw the boy's meaning at once, but Da Silva (to whom the allusion was of course a riddle) said with a puzzled air :

" May I ask to what the young Senhor is referring ? "

Eric told briefly his vision of the goblin face and the strange look of fierce joy cast by it at Jenor-Flan, and Dom Pablo's face waxed graver and graver at every word.

" This looks like foul play," he began, " and if so——"

" We must look into the matter at once, your Excellency is quite right," said the doctor.   " I presume the Senhor has already looked to see if there are any footmarks around the boy's hut."

" Not yet, Senhor," replied the other, looking rather foolish as he realized that this was the very first thing which he ought to have done.

" With your leave, then, Senhor Dom Pablo, I shall have the honour of examining the place along with you."

" With all my heart, Senhor Doutor " (Mr Doctor), said the other, bowing, " and

I trust your gracious indulgence will be pleased to forget the hasty words of a peevish old man."

Strong received the apology quite readily, and off set the whole four to the scene of action.

Dom Pablo's house (at which the boys looked with no small interest, having never been there before) was a large old-fashioned mansion of the Moresco-Spanish type, with the usual " azotea " or flat roof, and a " patio " (courtyard) in the centre, upon which most of the windows opened. Behind it lay the stables, outhouses, and servants' quarters, enclosed in a high wooden palisade, which, coupled with the strong walls and battlemented roof of the old house, and the few narrow, loophole-like windows which were all that could be seen from the outside, gave to the whole place quite the look of a fortress.

As soon as they arrived, to work went the doctor and Da Silva to search the ground of

E

the enclosure in quest of tell-tale footmarks, but all in vain. The earth around Jenor-Flan's hut was trodden hard, having for some weeks past had no rain to soften it, and even where it was less firm, whatever footprints might have been there had been trampled out by the passing to and fro of Da Silva's black servants in search of the missing lad.

But, whatever Dr Strong might inwardly feel with regard to all this bungling, he let no sign of it appear on his face, and only suggested, as calmly as ever, that they should now go round the palisade on the outside and see if they could find there any trace to guide them.

No sooner said than done, and with them went the two boys.

" I've found the trail ! " called out Dick all at once, from a part of the stockade farthest from the house and nearest to the lost boy's hut.

The others ran up to the spot, and there,

sure enough, plainly marked in the soil at the foot of the palisade, were several prints of bare feet, evidently those of negroes. These could not, it was certain, have been made by Dom Pablo's blacks, none of whom had been out of the enclosure that night, and, moreover, they would of course have come to it by the door.

"Well done, Dick!" cried Strong; "now let us see where these fellows came from, whoever they were."

The trail, when followed, seemed to lead up the slope as if coming from the shore, and though the footmarks were few and far between, there were enough of them to enable the doctor (who, thanks to his East Indian travels, was no mean tracker himself) to make another and a yet more important discovery. Some of the footprints, instead of pointing to the house, were turned toward the beach, as if these night prowlers had come back the same way as they went!

When he announced this discovery, Dick

could contain himself no longer, and broke out excitedly :

" Eric ! the black crew—the brigantine, you know."

" What *do* you mean, my boy ? " asked the doctor, staring at him, as did Da Silva likewise.

Dick told in a few words their strange adventure of the past night, not forgetting to mention that the mysterious vessel had sent a boat ashore ; to all which Dr Strong (who, as has been said, had heard nothing of it till then) listened with quite as serious a face as Dom Pablo himself.

" It looks to me more like kidnapping than murder," said he at last ; " for if they had killed him, they would not take the trouble to carry off his body, and we should have found it by now. But why on earth should anyone want to kidnap him ? "

To this no one had any answer, but, coupling the face seen by Eric in the thicket with the sending ashore of a boat by the black crew of the brigantine, Strong's guess seemed probable enough; and it was doubly confirmed by the fact that the footprints seen so far were all those of men, the smaller foot of the lad being nowhere visible, as if his supposed kidnappers had carried him in their arms and not allowed him to set foot on ground at all.

But their discoveries were not yet at an end, even now.

The trail led them right down to the shore, to a tiny strip of sand-beach close to the jutting point behind which the boys had seen the brigantine's boat vanish; and here lay plain to view the furrow made by a boat's keel that seemed to have been beached there, beside which, among a number of larger footmarks, was the unmistakable print of the boy prince, recognized by our heroes from the peculiar dint made by a slightly deformed toe on Jenor-Flan's left foot.

"Kidnapped, beyond a doubt!" said the doctor emphatically; "but why, I wonder?"

"Maybe they did it for the sake of his magic chain," hinted Dick.

What the boy meant as a joke, Da Silva took quite seriously, and he murmured in a rueful tone:

"Yes, that must have been it; I shall never see that magic necklace again."

"The old chap seems to take the loss of the chain a deal more to heart than the death of the boy, if he *is* dead!" whispered Eric to his chum, who answered only with a schoolboy grin.

"Well, Senhor Dom Pablo," said Strong, "there is nothing more for us to do, I think, except, indeed, to report the whole affair to the local authorities; for it would not be to your credit to pass over such a thing in silence."

"You say well, Senhor Dom Jorgé (George). I will do so forthwith."

He did so, and the authorities "took their usual measures," *i.e.* did nothing at all. But whatever they had done, it would have made no difference, for neither Jenor-Flan himself, nor the mysterious black crew who were supposed to have carried him off, were ever seen in Madeira again ; and Dr Strong, whether he liked or not, was left still in possession of the famous necklace of shells.

Along the brow of the cliff, like chimney ornaments ranged on a giant mantelpiece, stood five or six houses and store-sheds, with the white walls, broad overhanging roofs, and spacious verandas that mark all European dwellings in West Africa. To the right of these was a neat little church, outlining its snow-white belfry very prettily against the sea of green leaves and feathery tree-tops that filled up the background; and, high over all, more than ten thousand feet above the blue, sparkling sea from which it rose, the mighty summit of Clarence Peak soared up into the sky.

A year had gone by since the memorable night of Prince Jenor-Flan's disappearance, and had brought many changes in its train.

The mysterious " Black Prince " had not been seen or heard of since, and Strong had remained in possession of the famous shell necklace, not at all to his own satisfaction, for he could not bear the idea of having, even unintentionally, deprived the poor lad of the chain that he seemed to prize so highly. But the doctor himself was now quite another man; for his health had been so much improved by his stay at Madeira, that all that was needed to complete his cure was a long sea voyage, from which he was now coming back, having had a run out to the Cape and along the coast of Natal.

The boys were with him as usual, taller, stronger, browner, and more manly in every way; and both showed by the self-reliant look on their faces that they were fast acquiring that power of thinking for and helping themselves, which is one of the most valuable gifts that any boy can have.

But the greatest event of all is yet to be mentioned.

Dick's father, Colonel Fernott, had lately been achieving, in his new character as a British Commissioner on the West African

the morning," said the second officer of
their packet, Mr Jolly—who deserved his
name as fully as any man could do—"and,
if you like, I'll take you with me, and show
you one or two things that you might not
have time to find out for yourselves. We
don't sail till the day after to-morrow, so
I shall have time to pilot you about a bit.
Be ready at half-past five, sharp."

Such a chance was too good to lose;
and just as the sun peered above the
wood-crowned hills next morning, the three
voyagers and their friendly pilot shot away
from the ship's side as fast as four sturdy
Kroo oarsmen could drive them.

Mr Jolly had certainly chosen his time
well. The air was still delightfully cool,
and a fresh breeze was ruffling the wide
expanse of smooth sea and swaying the
broad, banner-like leaves of the vast host
of coco-palms and plantains which covered
the whole hill-side down to the very water's
edge.

But, before they had even set foot on the beach, the boys could discern ample proofs of that wasteful and destructive neglect by which Spain had been crippling the splendid resources of the finest island on the West African coast ever since she first took possession of it in 1778. The few buildings around the landing-place (whose half-rotten thatches were fast parting company with their mouldering planking) wore a look of chronic and undisguised slovenliness that told its own story. Out of the shallow water close to the beach started gauntly up a mass of rotting timbers that had once formed part of the hull of a gallant ship, which seemed to gaze at them through its empty ports with the blank, unseeing stare of a man born blind. The " quay " at which they landed was merely a rickety framework of battered, rusty iron plates (evidently taken from some dismantled steamer), every part of which was honeycombed with holes so many and so deep that any man who should venture on it in the dark would have little hope of escaping unhurt.

Just in front of this elegant pier the luxuriant woods that clothed the whole ridge from base to summit at every other point had been unsparingly hacked away, and two zigzag paths had been made up the hill, the one curving to the right and the other to the left.   At the point where they diverged yawned in the green hill-side a deep, low-browed archway, damp, black, and dismal as the mouth of a tunnel.

" Only a prison," remarked Mr Jolly coolly.   The boys, who shivered at the very idea of any human creature being immured in such a place, were greatly relieved when he added that it was no longer used ; but the broad, deep groove in the rock, that once held the ponderous door which had long since mouldered away, called up a ghastly vision of what might have happened on that spot a century before.   For in those days a Spanish colonial governor held irresponsible power, and might conveniently forget the doomed wretch whom he had prisoned in this horrible vault, till famine or the teeth of hungry rats had done their work, and left but a few whitening bones in mute witness of the nameless horrors that had been.

"These chaps aren't the regular people of the island, you know," said their guide, as three or four tall negroes, neatly clad in white, went by them with a civil greeting in English; "these are Kroo boys, imported from the West Coast. The island folks live more up among the hills, and I doubt if we shall fall in with any of 'em to-day. The white men call 'em 'Boobies,' because, when they meet a stranger, they sing out 'Booby,' which is only as if we should say 'Good morning,' though of course it doesn't sound very polite. But you can't get 'em to do a stroke of work at any price, and so the Spaniards have to get Kroo boys from the West Coast instead."

F

" These Kroo boys seem to have learned English pretty well," said Strong.

" Well, you see, this place where we are now is the most English part of the whole island.   We had a regular supply-station here in 1827, for the British cruisers that were running up and down the coast after Portugee slavers; but the place turned out unhealthy, and the Spaniards made a fuss about our being there on their ground, and so we gave it up.   Then, after a while, some English missionaries came and settled there, and started a school for the natives.   But after a time the Spaniards began bothering them in all sorts of ways.   They wouldn't let 'em teach English in their school, and they told them to ring their bells and sing their psalms quietly so as they could not be heard outside, and at last they forbade 'em to go on with the school at all."

Mr Jolly wound up his explanation by pointing out the ex-mission, a snug little white building with the usual overhanging eaves, long, low front, and shady veranda, standing in a pretty garden close behind the church.   Just outside its trim palisade the earth was overspread with clustering plants, which at once drew Dr Strong's attention by their dainty fern-like leaves, and tiny pink flowers, exactly like miniature deck-swabs made of floss-silk.

" I say, Ric," cried Dick Fernott, " if these flowers were yellow instead of pink, I should take 'em for the blossoms of that precious acacia that gave us such a time on the South African veldt.   Do you remember how the thorns used to pull us up at every turn ?   No wonder the Boers call 'em ' wait-a-bit ! ' "

" Ah, this is something very different," said Jolly, with a sly smile; "just touch one of 'em and you'll see."

Dick did so, and instantly the fairy leaflets shrank away from his touch with an almost human shudder, and folded themselves up as if avoiding pollution.

" The Sensitive Plant ! " cried Eric Wyse gleefully.

" That's it, sure enough," laughed their guide, " and I suppose this is the first time you have come across it."

It was so, and both lads were so taken up with the new wonder that Jolly had to remind them of the mounting sun and the growing heat before they could be got to move on.

In fact, the hardest part of their morning's work was yet to come. African roads are in some points very like African rivers, though the former often contain by far the more water of the two. Near the mouth of a road, before quitting the street that forms its estuary, it is usually broad and straight enough to be quite navigable. But as you ascend its channel, the road dwindles to a path, and the path to a goat-track, till, by the time you near its source, you need a microscope to find out whether you are on the road or off it.

Nor was this all. The path that the party were following was as slippery as a skating-rink from the recent rains; and whenever it mounted a steep rise or sloped suddenly down into a hollow, they had much ado to keep from going sprawling on their backs at every step.

But their toil was speedily and fully repaid. Hardly had they got clear of the " town " (which was smaller than many an English hamlet) when they plunged into a magnificent grove of mangoes, the dark foliage of which, forming a perfect arch overhead, toned down the bright tropical sunlight to a rich summer gloom of purple twilight, which harmonized well with the solemn silence of this great cathedral of nature.

And now the fierce fullness of tropical life poured out all its wonders around them in measureless abundance. The flag-like plantain and the plumy coco-palm, the white trumpet-shaped moon-flower, the orange-tree with its golden fruit shining like midnight stars amid its dark, glossy leaves ; the spiky pine-apple, the bayonet-like " croc-chien," the paw-paw with its green hanging globes ; the broad-leaved, white-blossomed frangipani, wasting on this lonely forest the exquisite perfume for which civilized Europe pays a high price ; the six-fingered leaf of the cassava—bread and potato in one—which once did good service to me and my shipmates in the gloomy days that followed our shipwreck at the mouth of Cestos River ; the graceful bread-fruit, crested with fan-like tufts of dark-green foliage; and, high over all, the stately ceiba, a born prince of the forest, with his buttress-like roots struck deep into the soft, rich soil below, and his vast, branching head set like a crown on the smooth, straight, pillar-like stem that towers many feet above the tallest of the encircling giants.

" Fancy an English schoolboy turned

loose here!" chuckled Dr Strong, with a sly glance from his boy-comrades to the riotous abundance around, "in a region where pine-apples grow wild like black-berries, and banana-palms are so thick that you can hardly squeeze in between, and one's foot slips on ripe coco-nuts and bread-fruits at every step, and mangoes and oranges lie rolling in the dirt like stones at home!"

"If he were," said Dick with a grin, "I should think he'd die of indigestion before he had been here a week!"

At that moment a shout from Jolly made them leap back just in time to avoid an advancing army of the terrible "driver-ants" that spare neither man nor beast, and, in fact, made short work, before their very eyes, of a huge centipede that was trailing its black shining length, like a strip of velvet, over the yellow clay into the grass beyond. That brown bulging excres-cence in the fork of a tree above Dick's

head, which looked so harmless, was an
ants' nest, swarming with busy and ferocious
life.   Farther on, the boys espied a palm,
whose coco-nuts, instead of growing in the
usual way, appeared to have ranged themselves at regular intervals along the slender,
tapering stems from which the leaves had
been completely torn away.   But a second
glance showed the seeming coco-nuts to be
really birds' nests, in the making of which
the missing leaves had been used up to the
last fibre.

These queer dwellings hung like bags
with the mouth downward, swaying to and
fro with every movement of the bough;
and a number of long-tailed birds, with
black heads and yellow bodies, kept flying
in and out of them with a great flapping
and screeching, as if (like certain far more
civilized creatures elsewhere) they were
bent on making the greatest possible amount
of noise and fuss over the smallest possible
amount of work.

But a far different sight awaited them farther on, the grim effect of which was deepened tenfold by its contrast with the merry native boys, and gaily painted plank huts, and cheery greetings, and bright, sunny life of the quaint little toy village through which they passed to reach it.

Beyond the village, their path began to wind amid forests of wild grass and thick dark clumps of thorny undergrowth, bringing them at last to the edge of a gloomy hollow overshadowed by huge trees, and half-choked with a riotous profusion of briars, knot-grass, lianas, ferns, fungi, and other vegetable outlaws. Amid that wilderness of hideous abundance lay a few neglected English graves, some still marked with crumbling head-stones and rusty iron rails, while others had already fallen away into mere shapeless mounds half-buried in trailing creepers.

With the sight of these monuments of death came back to them a haunting memory of the sad story told them by the captain only the day before :

"When we came out last year, we brought a missionary's wife with us, quite a young girl, with as sweet a face of her own as you'd see anywhere. She was looking forward to the new place and the new life just like a child, though it seemed to me she was rather young for the work she'd have to do. When we put her ashore, it was a regular picture to see her waving good-bye to us with her little bit of a hand-kerchief as she went up the steep path from the landing-place. But it was just the same old story ; she hadn't been there three days when she fell sick of fever, and her husband got scared, and promised that she should go home at once ; and as long as the poor girl had strength to sit up, she did nothing but watch and watch for our steamer to come back from the south and take her away. But when we did come, we came too late ; for, the very morning we sighted the island, the poor young thing died."

But a far more startling surprise was yet in store.

Dick had gone forward a step or two into the thinner brushwood, to see if it hid any other graves which they might have overlooked, when there came a sharp crackle in the thicket, and up started, right in front of him, a tattered, haggard, ghastly form, the gaunt black face of which (for the figure was that of a negro) was so distorted with mingled terror and rage as to be scarcely human!

CHAPTER VI

BAD NEWS

ALL Dick's firmness could not repress a cry of amazement at this startling apparition, which at once brought all the rest to the spot, hastily asking what was the matter. At the sight of them, and the sound of their voices, the hobgoblin's convulsed face cleared visibly, and he said in broken English, with an air of relief :

" Inglis man good ; no hurt black man."

"We shall not hurt you, you may be quite sure of that ! " said Dr Strong heartily ; " but who are you, and what are you doing here ? "

The negro's story was soon told. He was one of the victims of the system of bringing black labourers from the mainland as if for a few years, and then keeping them there altogether—in fact, making actual slaves of the poor fellows, who had no chance of escape with the sea all round them, ignorant as they were even of the direction in which their native country lay.

Having managed to slip away undetected by his master, he had taken refuge in the bush, meaning to lie hid till dark, and then to steal down to the harbour, seize one of the boats that were lying there, and make for the nearest British gunboat, on which he knew he would be safe.

The boys flushed with indignant surprise at the idea of such things being done on a sea swept by British ships, and fringed with British colonies; and as the tale ended, Dick called out excitedly :

" Right you are, Johnny ; no one dare touch you under the old Union Jack ! "

" No, I have a better plan than that," said Jolly, who had listened with silent attention. " This man wants to get back to the Ivory Coast, and these gunboats may cruise about for a year without going near it. Now, I happen to know that the captain of your Portuguese boat wants hands, for he asked me last night where he could get some; and I am sure he'd take this man gladly, and ask no questions."

"If he does ask any, trust me to stop his mouth!" said Strong grimly; "he won't want to quarrel with a friend of Colonel Fernott."

At the mention of Fernott's name, the runaway black's eyes sparkled.

"Him good man, Cunnel Fernott; friend ob my tribe!"

An eager query was on Dick Fernott's lips, but Jolly checked him, and said:

"Are you anything of a sailor, my man?"

"Me go two voyage in Inglis ship, one time."

Jolly nodded approvingly, and proceeded to suggest that they should leave the refugee the food they had brought with them, come back at nightfall with a sailor-suit for him, and put him at once aboard his new vessel. This was done; and the very next day saw the travellers and their black recruit clear of the island.

For the first few days all went well; and they learned with great interest in one of their talks with the rescued black, Kabembi, that he was a Jaloofa, one of the very tribe whose dispute with the Mbantus over the debatable land Colonel Fernott was just then engaged in settling.

The weather continued fine till they sighted the mouth of the Calabar River, when the rain and mist of the fatal " Fever Coast " began in earnest ; and through that leaden, ghostly dimness, the dreary pano-rama looked doubly ghastly. Beneath that frightful amphibious forest, look as they might, there was no sign of land. The gaunt white roots started up like skeletons from the black, slimy waters into which the drooping branches dipped their dark, leathery leaves; and through the few breaks in the wall of tangled boughs nothing could be seen but a maze of black pools and miry creeks, winding farther and farther into the dismal labyrinth till they were lost in the deeper shadows beyond.

Down the broad, sluggish, oily-brown stream came slowly to meet them a long train of floating islets (some of considerable size) formed of earth and wild grass, and even bushes, torn from the soft bank by the current. To this marvel was soon added another—a great number of oysters on the roots and hanging boughs along the water's edge.

"That looks like Baron Munchausen," laughed Strong, "but it only means that the oysters cling to the trees at high tide, and are left bare by the ebb. It is a pet joke here to persuade a greenhorn that oysters picked fresh from the trees on which they grow are a great local dainty."

On they steamed, and a burst of ear-splitting screams from the wooded islet which they were passing fully bore out its name of Parrot Island. A little farther on came flitting toward them, through mist and rain, like a messenger of hope, a splendid tropical butterfly, quite as big as a young sparrow, on whose outspread wings a faint gleam of returning sunshine made a halo of golden glory. The rain ceased, the mist cleared, the plumy crests of stately palms began to mingle with the foul, snaky mangroves of the swamp; and as they swung round a sharp bend, and the bang of their signal-gun fired a long train of thundering echoes among the surrounding hills, Duke Town itself came in sight in the distance, on the left bank of the river.

The well-built wharves and factories along the water's edge, the steamers at anchor in front of them, the trim white buildings of the Mission dotted here and

G

there amid the dark foliage that clad the nearest of the two flanking hills, gave the spot, at first sight, quite a civilized aspect. But one glance at the shadowy mass of forest piled up into the very sky just behind it (in which a recent landslip had left a bare patch of ghastly red, like the scar of a raw wound) sufficed to show that barbarism still held its own, though Europe had long been encamped in its midst.

The town possessed one public monument—a somewhat remarkable one.

As they neared the wharf of the European trading factory, the boys noticed a figure hanging from one of the posts that supported its ample roof. At the first glance one might have taken it for the gibbeted corpse of a very badly-dressed pirate with an unnaturally long neck ; but a second look showed it to be a " dummy " stuffed with straw—Africa's first attempt at a Guy Fawkes. The head was represented

by a round wooden ball, painted black and
surmounted by a grey felt hat, with a very
dirty white cloth twisted round it by way
of a sunshade. A brass pan formed the
shoulders, two small bells hung from the
arms and a third from the waist; and
a flowing drapery of red cotton handkerchiefs made a gallant but vain attempt to
hide the fact that this statue (like the
fabulous bird of Eastern legend) had no
legs !

But the gem of this singular monument
was its inscription.

A large square paper on its breast kept
in countenance a second on its back, and
both bore the same legend in staring black
letters :

> " NOTICE.—Prince Eyambo has
> owed me four (4) puns (puncheons
> of palm-oil) this last four (4)
> years, and will not pay me. Be-
> ware of him ! "

CHAPTER VII

AN UNSEEN ENEMY

IT may be imagined with what crushing force this terrible news fell upon the boys and their guardian, who had already thought Colonel Fernott as good as safe at home, instead of being actually in the worst peril of his whole life.

They eagerly questioned the agent, but he had really very little to add to what he had already told.

It appeared that the Colonel's decision in the dispute between the Jaloofas and the Mbantus had been against the latter ; and they, whether of set purpose or in a sudden burst of fury, had fallen upon him, overpowered his native escort, and carried him away captive to their own capital—no pleasant news for the travellers after all the tales of Mbantu cruelties that they had heard from their Jaloofa friend Kabembi, who was not likely to speak well of a tribe that had always been the enemy of his own.

But there was still some comfort left them. Kabembi himself, when appealed to, positively declared that the Mbantus, savage as they were, would never be such fools as to kill so important a prisoner. There could be no doubt that they meant (as the agent had said) to force him to reverse his decision against them, and as long as there was, or they thought there was, any hope of doing so, his life was quite safe.

This, however, was but cold comfort at the best, for all three knew the Colonel too well to think for a moment that he would ever let himself be bullied into an act of injustice, and, in the meantime, he was away inland, far beyond their reach, and how were they to get him back?

Nor was Kabembi himself without a secret anxiety of his own. He had already shown himself to be so handy and able a seaman, that it was more than doubtful if the captain would let him go when they reached the port where he wished to land. In a word, the whole pleasure of the voyage was now spoiled for all the four, and their one thought was to get it over as quickly as they could.

It was shortened for them, however, by the fact that, at three or four of the lesser ports, they found it impossible to have any communication with the shore at all, and were forced to run right past—no rare thing in West Africa, where, even in the calmest weather, the breaking of the great waves on the beach is at times so heavy and dangerous that no boat can dare to land or put off, and any failure to land or bring away cargo is fully accounted for by the expressive local phrase of " a bad beach."

In their burning impatience to get forward, our lads hardly noticed the queer little stations dotted along the flat, sandy beach, between the boundless forest on one side and the boundless sea on the other; and the chief impression left on their minds by this part of the Guinea Coast was that of an endless dish of parsley edged with an equally endless smear of mustard; and the creeks and rivers which, at long intervals, broke the benumbing sameness of the shore seemed to indicate that (as Dick spitefully said) "Afric's sunny fountains" had got tired of "rolling down their golden sand," and had taken to roll down some very dirty water instead.

But at Accra, on the Gold Coast, a sight was in store for them which interested them in spite of themselves.

Soon after sunrise they saw the bold rocky headland of Winnebah thrusting forth its broad black breast into the roaring sea, as if defying the utmost fury of the white-lipped breakers that came thundering against it, flinging their great hills of foam mast-high into the air, while, amid the rocks above, four small white houses peered down into the howling chaos like watching children, half pleased and half frightened.

"Come, that's something like!" cried the admiring Dick, brightening up. "It's quite a treat to see a bit of high ground again, instead of that horrid old flat, bristly jungle, that looks just like a second-hand hair-brush a hundred miles long."

An hour later, two or three long, sloping hills began to loom through the breaking mist, and suddenly, as if at the rising of a curtain, the trim white houses of Accra and the bold ridge of dark-red sandstone on which they stood, and the tall, feathery palms that rose above them against the skyline, and the curving, yellow beach below with its ring of glittering foam, and the wide green uplands beyond, ending in the rocky headland crowned with the low, massive wall of the old Danish fort of Christiansborg, all started into view at once.

But hardly had they sighted it, when it became clear that some great event was exciting the whole town to the utmost.

The entire shore was one flutter of gay flags, from the landing-place right up to Christiansborg Castle; the rising wind brought the stirring music of a native military band; shouting crowds of blacks, in all the colours of the rainbow (some of whom wore huge grass hats that hid them almost to the waist), were eddying to and fro among the tiny mud-huts with their top-heavy thatches of dried grass, and the tumble-down plank sheds that looked like overgrown packing-cases with one side knocked out; and as the boys were watching, a puff of smoke burst from one of the seven long iron guns planted on the brow of the cliff, and a sharp report awoke all

against ten times their number of savage Awoonas till their ammunition was spent, and had then charged home with the bayonet, and swept away their swarming enemies like dust.

They were evidently awaiting the governor, nor had they long to wait; for by this time he and his officers had scrambled down into their boat, and, even as the boys looked, the boat shot out from the ship's side and away he went to see whether he was to be drowned or not.

Up and down, up and down went the adventurous boat, now rising far into the air on a hill-top of seething foam, now plunging with a dizzy swing into the depths of a shadowy green valley between two towering walls of dark water. Every moment it seemed as if they must certainly be overwhelmed by some huge roller that came rushing on, curling its vast, snowy crest far above their heads like a falling avalanche. But the monster always missed them by a hair's-breadth, for the gaunt, black scare-crows who sat perched along the rocking gunwale, each with one foot in a kind of stirrup of rope fixed in the boat's side, had no match on the whole Guinea Coast for such work as this.

Every stroke of the short, strong paddles (which, instead of being spear-pointed like those of the Grain Coast, or spoon-shaped like those of the Niger, resembled a clumsy three-pronged fork with very broad and thick points) was accompanied by a sharp howl such as Mr Lowell used to call a "dog-solo-gy," and at times even by a few words of untranslatable abuse hurled with angry gestures at the furious waves. Meanwhile scores of eager eyes were watching their progress both from the ship and from the shore; but, save when flung up on the crest of a huge billow, both men and boat were quite invisible from either point.

When they did become visible again, they were seen to be no longer heading for the beach, but running parallel with it just outside the great battle-line of gnashing foam, and seemingly watching for a break in it through which they might slip just at the right moment. If they could do so, they were safe; if not, the boat must capsize to a certainty.

Louder and wilder grew the shouts of the rowers, quicker and quicker the paddle-strokes, and all at once the boat was seen to turn and go right at the line of furious breakers. At the same moment came a rush down the beach of half a dozen brawny blacks, who dashed into the whirling foam on one side just as the boat entered it on the other.

For an instant all was lost in a storm of flying spray; and then, as the boat ran high up the beach, the half-dozen negroes were seen to rush in, seize the great official by wrist and ankle, and carry him ashore like a baby!

The boys laughed in spite of themselves;

but the excitement of this strange scene was not over yet.

All seemed already safe, when a mighty wave rushed far up the beach and broke over the governor and his bearers with a thud that was plainly heard on the steamer. Down went governor, negroes and all, sprawling on their backs on the wet sand amid a whirl of foam, and the great man himself fairly turned head-over-heels, as if he were trying to jump down his own throat. A roar of laughter burst from the whole crowd, and the governor, springing to his feet again, laughed as heartily as any one, like a sensible fellow as he was.

Strong had intended to land in turn, see the governor himself, and find out what could be done toward rescuing Colonel Fernott, but the steamer's agent (who came off a little later in a native surf-boat) told him that the local authorities were already informed of the whole affair, and had

H

promptly taken measures to aid the prisoner;
so our voyagers, when they sailed again on
the evening of the following day, did so
with much lighter hearts.

The Jaloofa, too, was in high spirits as
they drew nearer and nearer to the point
whence he hoped to reach his own land;
and he confided to the boys (who heard him
with visible dismay) that if the captain
would not let him go he meant to jump
overboard and swim ashore, taking his
chance of the sharks!

But now the good luck that had gone
with them so long began to change. The
bright sunshine faded, the mist and rain of
that dismal region closed round them like
a pall and the wind was fast rising to a gale,
and the experienced doctor knew well what
a gale might mean on that perilous coast,
where, within the last three days, they
had sighted no fewer than five dismasted
wrecks—an ominous hint of what might
be their own fate in that frail little vessel,

which, moreover, was sorely in need of repair.

Nor was this Strong's only cause of anxiety.

Now that the whole purpose of their voyage had been so suddenly overturned, what were they to do ?   To go on to Madeira and England, leaving his best friend in deadly peril without an effort to save him, was an idea that the brave man could not abide ; but, on the other hand, if he landed at the nearest British settlement to the scene of action (which was what he would have wished to do), the boys must either go on to Madeira by themselves, with a captain and crew whom the doctor privately thought far from trustworthy, or they must remain for an indefinite time on the sickliest part of the whole African coast at the imminent risk of dying of fever !

Look at it which way he would, it seemed a hopeless dilemma ; but the question, little as he dreamed of it, was about to be settled for him in a way that no man living could have foreseen.

Cape Coast Castle, Elmina, Cape Three Points slipped by them one by one, and they were already well up the Ivory Coast, when the hovering mist thickened round them to such a degree that, for all they could see to the contrary, they might have been in the middle of the Pacific or at the North Pole.

Dr Strong, knowing well how imperfectly all this part of the coast was laid down in the charts, and feeling certain that they were a good deal nearer to the land than was at all safe, ventured to give the captain a hint to that effect, but the latter gruffly replied that he could take care of his own vessel and needed no one to teach him his business.

But though he rejected so rudely the doctor's well-meant warning, it seemed to have had some effect on him all the same ;

for by and by he gave orders to slacken down to half-speed, and at half-speed they went all the rest of that day. Their slow progress, the dead silence around them, the engulfing dimness on every side and the spectral aspect of the crew as their figures loomed through it half-seen, inspired Dick Fernott to remark—in a very bold flight of fancy for him—that they seemed like a boat full of dead men on their way to be buried.

The two lads recalled later on, with but too good reason (though they thought little of it at the time), that the Portuguese captain, who happened to be passing just as Dick made this remark, and knew enough English to understand it, started visibly as he heard the words, and, turning angrily on the boy, fiercely told him to hold his tongue and not talk such nonsense, and then tramped off ere the startled lad could reply.

"What on earth is the matter with

him ? " asked Dick, staring after him in amazement, " he must have got out of bed the wrong leg foremost."

" Hush, my boy ! " said the doctor gravely. " Let him alone ; you see he is not in a mood to be talked to. I heartily wish this voyage of ours were over ! "

The tone in which he spoke the last words startled both lads even more than the words themselves.

" Hullo ! " cried Dick, looking at him in surprise, " it's a new thing for you, Uncle George, to talk like that ! "

" You don't think anything is going to go wrong with us, do you ? " asked Eric.

" Never mind what I think ! " said Strong, in a tone of impatience very rare with him, " least said soonest mended."

That night Dick Fernott (who had gone to bed rather later than usual) had a strange and troubled dream.

He dreamed that they were at anchor close to the shore, under the shadow of a great mountain; and he knew (he could not tell how) that on the other side of it his father was standing, and that it was about to fall down and crush him, unless some one could warn him in time.

The boy struggled frantically to leap into the sea and carry the warning himself, but he seemed to be spellbound, for strive as he might, he could not stir hand or foot —could not even cry out. Then, all at once, he saw the mountain begin to tremble, and its tremor shook him even where he stood. Again it quivered—then it bowed to one side, with a long, grating, grinding noise; then came another shock, as it leaped from its place and fell with a mighty crash, so loud and terrific that the dreamer started and awoke.

As he did so, there came a third shock, which made the light vessel quiver from stem to stern, and then followed a rush of water and a wild clamour of hoarse voices and hurrying steps overhead, and the captain was heard to shout :

" All on deck there ! all on deck ! "

It was the felon stab of an unseen enemy.   The ship had struck on a rock and was sinking !

CHAPTER VIII

THE COMING OF THE DESTROYERS

THE hanging lamp in the cabin had flown in pieces as the vessel struck, and all was dark, and amid the gloom, there began a noise and confusion that no words could convey. The trampling of feet overhead, the shouts of the seamen calling to each other, the cracking and grinding of the broken timbers, the hiss and gurgle of the water as it flowed in, the battering of the waves against the reeling hull, the roar of the escaping steam, the crash and rattle of chairs, boxes and benches dashed hither and thither by every plunge of the sinking ship, made a maddening din.[1]

In such a case, any man might have

[1] Most of the details in this and the following chapters are taken from a shipwreck of my own on the West African coast.—D.K.

been pardoned for losing his head for a moment, much more two untried boys of fourteen.

But, strange to say, they were not flurried in the least ; and Dr Strong himself, now that he was actually face to face with the peril that he had foreseen, appeared to have quite shaken off his former agitation, and was as cool and brave as ever.

The fact was that this sudden awakening from sleep to find the ship sinking under them was so startling and unnatural, that the boys could not realize it just at first. It seemed to them as if all this were happening to some one else, and they were only looking on.

Had they been able fairly to take in the fact that they were wrecked on one of the wildest parts of the whole African coast, with the certainty (as it seemed) of being either swallowed by the sea, or killed (and perhaps eaten) by black savages, their courage might have failed; but, as it was, they saw only that the first thing to be done was to dress and get on deck as fast as they could, and both lads hurried on their clothes as quickly as the pitch black gloom would let them.

"Where's Jenor-Flan's shell chain?" cried Eric all at once, "we had it out last night, you know. We must not leave that behind, at any price!"

"Never mind it now, my boy," cried Strong, "what we have got to do is to save our own lives, not to bother about picking things up."

"All right, I have it!" called out Eric, as he groped out the chain and put it round his own neck. "Where are you, Uncle George? I can't see a bit!"

"Here I am, come this way, and let us get on deck as quick as we can."

This, however, was easier said than done, for the water-logged hull had settled down so much on one side, that going up the companion ladder was like climbing the side of a house. When they did at last manage to clamber up, it took some time to get the door open, and just as they came out on deck, Dr Strong heard a gruff voice call out :

" Well, if you won't come, stay there and be drowned along with them ! "

Strong's heart sank as he listened, for the voice was that of the captain, and it seemed to come from below ! With a nameless fear tightening round his bold heart, the brave man clutched the quarter rail, and made his way by it hand over hand, along the rocking, reeling deck, only to find his worst fears confirmed. A faint gleam of moonlight had just broken through the driving clouds, showing him that the deck was empty, and that one of the ship's boats, crowded with men, was already two lengths away from her side, and getting farther every moment !

" As I thought ! " said the doctor grimly ;

" the sneaks have run away and left us to drown."

" Me no run 'way, Massa Doctor," said Kabembi's voice at his side ; " you berry good to me—me stay and help you all me can."

" Well done, Kabembi ! you're a brick ! " cried Dick Fernott heartily ; " and, after all, it doesn't matter much, for we have another boat here still."

" Dat oder boat no good, Massa Dick —rotten all same squashed banana ! "

It was indeed so, and Dick's face fell visibly, but just then Strong said to him very gravely :

" We are safer where we are, Dick ; now that this craft is firmly fixed on the rock, I don't think she will sink any farther, unless she were to slide right off it. We may be very thankful, I can tell you, that those fellows didn't wait and take us with them, for I am sure their boat can never live in such a sea, overcrowded as she is."

And, in fact, it soon appeared that he was right.

The wind had begun to fall, but the sea went higher than ever, and as the moon grew brighter and brighter (for the storm was now abating), the boat was seen to be labouring heavily, and making but little way in spite of the frantic efforts of her crew. In fact, it needed no great shrewdness to see that this unequal battle with death was already overtasking the strength of the rowers, and that, as soon as they failed to keep the boat's head to the waves, she would fall into the trough of the sea, and capsize to a certainty.

And now three monstrous billows came roaring on, so close together that to ride one without being caught in the trough of the next seemed quite impossible. Loud and wild rose the shouts of the struggling men, who set their teeth in dogged desperation as their frail little craft climbed up the vast hill of dark water like a fly on a wall.

"Pull for your lives!" roared Strong, just as if they could hear him, "before it can break and swamp you!"

Hurrah! they were over it ere the combing crest could overwhelm them, and down they plunged into the dark hollow below, with that dizzy, sickening swoop that haunts one in troubled dreams of falling headlong from a measureless height into a fathomless abyss. Up again, with the same rush and roar and yell, and the second wave was passed; and now came the hugest and most dangerous of all, with its foamy crest glimmering ghastly white in the fitful moonlight.

All at once Dr Strong, as he watched them, drew a short, quick breath, as if in sudden pain, for he had seen that they were a moment late in breasting this third wave, and he needed no one to tell him what must come of it.

In fact, the vast white crest began to curl over ere the boat could mount it, and the doomed bark vanished into the hollow of that monstrous wave as if plunging into a cavern. For a moment all was hid in seething foam, and then the boat was seen tossing, keel upward, on the mighty waves, but of her ill-fated crew nothing was ever seen again.

"May God have mercy on them!" said the man whom they had left to perish, casting a pitying glance out over the wild waters.

But just then, as if to be in harmony with the gloomy horror of that fearful retribution, the moon clouded over, and all was dark.

So long as the moonlight had lasted, the boys had been gazing fixedly to the northward, where the land must lie, in the hope of getting some idea, however faint, of the kind of coast on which they had been stranded. The Jaloofa, too (who knew that his own country lay somewhere in that direction), did the same, but all to no purpose. Neither the clear young eyes of the English lads, nor the keener sight of the African savage, could pierce the cloud of mist that brooded in that quarter over sea and sky. For all they could see to the contrary, they might have been a thousand miles from land instead of five or six.

The deck lanterns, like all the rest, had gone to pieces as the ship struck; but Strong, calling to mind a small lantern in the captain's deck-cabin, rummaged it out, lighted it, and looked at his watch.

"Five o'clock already," said he, as cheerily as ever; "it will be light in an hour more, and then we can see where we are."

"And what are we to do, Uncle George?" asked Dick.

"Well, as soon as it's light enough to see what we're about, we'll patch up that other boat—or, if we can't, make a raft—

I

seizing his arm, "keep quiet, whatever you do."

"What? aren't we to make any fight, then, Uncle George?" said Dick Fernott, whose blood was up at once at the idea of tamely letting himself be butchered without one struggle for his life.

"Mustn't think of it!" said the doctor, who had learned a good deal about the ways of African savages from his own travels, and still more from Colonel Fernott's letters to him. "Sit down and keep quite still—it is our only chance, and, with God's help, I trust we shall get through it yet."

In fact it was clear that nothing was to be gained by resisting, for they could see that the coming destroyers were at least forty strong, and all armed with spears, knives, or hatchets, and not a few with guns as well.

The boys, taking it for granted that Uncle George must know best, sat down upon the only spot on the slanting deck

that could give them any support, the
hatch of the little cabin. Dr Strong took
his seat beside them, and Kabembi stood
behind the group, giving it the air of three
white chiefs with a black slave.

On came the savages, with shrill cries of
ferocious joy, as they saw how utterly at
their mercy the helpless ship was.

The sea, though now going down fast,
tossed the canoes to and fro and flung them
about like toys, but the wonderful skill of
those who handled them at length brought
them right alongside of the wreck.

In a moment more the flood of wild forms
and gaunt, wolfish faces, and brandished
weapons, came pouring over the deck.

CHAPTER IX

PRISONERS

It might well have been expected that the savages, as soon as they gained the deck, would have killed the four defenceless castaways on the spot, and then have set to work at once to plunder the ship ; and this was what, in any ordinary case, they would certainly dave done.

But Dr Strong's knowledge of savages and their ways had stood him in good stead, and the wisest thing for him to do was just what he had done.

Like all barbarous races, the blacks of the West African coast, when they meet with a man who does not seem to be afraid of them in the least, are always inclined to be afraid of him ; and just so it was now. Confounded by the utter stillness and perfect composure of the castaways, the assailants came to a sudden halt, and for a few moments the four voyagers and the forty intruders looked fixedly at each other, without a word spoken on either side.

In truth the savages were quite at a loss what to say or do ; for the perfect calmness of these seemingly helpless strangers, who did not even move at their coming, and appeared to care as little for them as if they had not been there at all, was quite a new thing in their experience, and they did not know what to make of it.

To be so perfectly cool in the face of seemingly certain death, the white men must have some means of defence of which their enemies knew nothing, and who could tell what it might be ? Would they, by the power of magic, fling the whole gang back into the sea again, or had they a store of gunpowder on board, by setting fire to which they could blow into the air, in one moment, themselves and their foes together? Who could say what a white man might or might not do?

It was the best proof of the deep impression which had been made on these fierce plunderers, that not one of them seemed even to have noticed the Jaloofa, plain as he was to view, all their attention was taken up with the "white magicians"—for such they evidently took our heroes to be.

At last a tall, bony fellow with a fearfully scarred face, who seemed to be the leader of the band, ventured to step cautiously forward, very much like a child venturing up to a very large and savage dog, which might at any moment spring up and bite it. But ere he could speak, a sudden movement of Eric's head revealed to him the famous "magic" shell chain, which the boy had put round his neck when the ship struck, to save it from being left behind.

Had the chain been a loaded cannon pointed right at his head, the savage could hardly have looked more confounded. He started back so hastily that he all but fell, and stared with a look of blank bewilderment at the necklace and its wearer, while his men, who seemed quite as much startled as himself, looked meaningly at each other, and whispered excitedly among themselves.

The tall chief, in his turn, exchanged a few words with his followers, and then, facing round again, turned to Eric and said something with great energy, which Dr Strong rightly guessed to be an inquiry how the chain had come into his hands. But as none of them (not even the Jaloofa) understood a word of the tongue in which the questioner spoke, he could only reply by uttering, as distinctly as he could, the name of Jenor-Flan.

The mention of this name had an even more marked effect than the sight of the chain itself. The chief repeated it aloud, his men echoed it, and the look of wonder on their faces now became tinged with

an expression of manifest pleasure, which
visibly softened their grim visages for the
first time.

What all this meant, our heroes could
not even guess.　That the possession of the
necklace had done them a service in some
way was clear enough, but what it was,
or how it had been done, they were quite
at a loss to imagine.　The boys were
completely puzzled ; and even Dr Strong
himself could only conjecture vaguely that
these savages must be as firm believers as
Jenor-Flan himself in the magic power of
the chain, and that they meant to stipulate
for its being given up to them as the price
of their prisoners' lives.

"Can you make out anything of what
they say, Kabembi ? " asked he.

"No sabbee (know) one word, Massa
Doctor," said the Jaloofa, shaking his head.
"No my people, dem feller ; me tink dey
Maloja man."

Maloja ! where had Strong heard that

name before ?   He pondered, but nothing came of it.

To the boys, too, it seemed familiar, though they could not tell how ; very likely Dick's father might have mentioned it in some of his letters.

But, in any case, it might be as well to find out if Kabembi's guess were a true one, and Dr Strong, turning to the chief, pointed right at him and said inquiringly : " Maloja ? "

" Maloja, Maloja ! " replied the tall man, with a pleased smile; and several of his men, pressing forward in turn, pointed to themselves and called out :

" Maloja, Maloja ! "

Strong was more puzzled than ever. Why should the bare fact of their knowing the name of the tribe have made such an impression on the savages, and an impression, too, which was plainly more favourable to them than anything that had passed yet ?

For a moment he was inclined to think

it merely a sudden outbreak of the vanity common to all savage races, which exulted in the idea that even strangers from over the sea had actually heard of them. But this idea was instantly thrust out by a sudden conviction (for which he could not account) that this new turn in their favour was in some way due to the mysterious chain, and that it must be either the tribal badge of the Malojas or an object of special reverence among them.

He was sorely tempted to satisfy himself on this point, too, by uttering the word " ju-ju " (magic) which the newcomers would be sure to understand, and pointing to the necklace ; but, like a sensible man as he was, he wisely resolved to give time for the good impression that he had evidently made to sink into the minds of his strange visitors, and not run the risk of weakening it by a false step of any kind.

In fact, it soon appeared that they were not wholly safe, even now.

The tall chief called out from among his followers three men (evidently persons of note like himself) and conferred with them apart in a low tone, as if he did not wish the rest to hear what was said.

Our heroes easily guessed that it was their fate which was being decided by this debate, and naturally watched it with much interest ; but as they knew nothing of the language used by the speakers, they were reduced to studying the debaters' faces, in the hope of thus getting some clue to their meaning.

Nor was this hard to do ; for the latter's expressive looks and emphatic gestures spoke for themselves, and the English easily made out that while the tall leader and one of the others seemed to be on their side, the two remaining speakers were plainly adverse to them, one of the two—a short, broad-chested, fierce-eyed man of middle age—being especially vehement against them.

But the conference did not last long. The tall chief seemed to make some suggestion, to which the two objectors agreed, and then the council broke up.

Then it suddenly occurred to Dr Strong that though their own lives were apparently safe for the present, the same security might not extend to Kabembi, whom the savages would be likely enough to kill either as a possible enemy or merely from their natural love of blood. He resolved, therefore, to claim the latter as under their protection, in the most unmistakable manner ; and rising from his seat (a movement at which the nearest savages drew back hastily) he laid one hand protectingly on the Jaloofa's shoulder, and with the other waved back the savages as if forbidding them to touch him.

The tall leader nodded as if assenting, and made the sign of peace by holding out both hands with the palms upward, and Kabembi's grim face (which had been set like a flint all through the debate) relaxed for the first time.

So far, so good; but what next? That their lives were safe, for the present at least, was clear enough, but what was to be done with them?

"What will they do with us, do you think, Uncle George?" asked Dick in a low voice.

"Take us with them as prisoners, I should say," replied Strong in the same tone. "It's a bad job, but I think we shall get through it yet."

The shrewd doctor took good care not to utter the thought which was in his mind at that moment—that not much was to be hoped from the kindness of men who, less than four years before, had stripped to the skin a wrecked German crew, and left them thus unprotected under the scorching sun till many of them were literally flayed alive, the skin peeling off as if from the action of boiling water.

But this was no time to speak of such things, and he spoke as cheerily as he could.

No comfort, however, was needed by the eager boys, who found this strange adventure very much to their taste. Like Robinson Crusoe, they had been shipwrecked; like him, they had met with real live savages, as picturesque and barbaric as his; and they were now going off to some unknown region, where, perhaps (who could say?) no white man had ever set foot till now! What more could heart desire?

Just then there was a great bustle among the Malojas, several of whom were seen to scramble back into the largest of the five canoes, and then the tall chief (whom his men called Karri) came up to the castaways with an air of marked respect, and invited them, by signs, to take their places in the boat.

They did so at once, and Kabembi followed them.

" What do you think they mean to do with us, Kabembi ? " whispered Strong to the Jaloofa, as they took their seats.

" Me tink dey bring us to de king, and he say what do to us."

The suggestion was a startling one, as tending to show that their lives were not safe even yet ; but it sounded probable enough, and Strong had no doubt that the man was right. Anyhow, there was no help for it—go they must, and in a few moments they were all settled in the stern of the canoe, so far as it could be said to have one. The crew, including Karri himself, got on board in turn, and the boat pushed off.

A second canoe followed a moment later ; but the crews of the other three remained behind to plunder the ship, a duty which they would have performed with equal zeal and handiness had death been staring them in the face ; for the West African savage is a born pillager, and will steal a sewing-

K

machine or a Latin dictionary for the mere pleasure of taking what does not belong to him.

Several miles of sea lay between the wreck and the shore, and even with some of the best paddlers on the whole coast to send them along, the boys had plenty of time to have a good look at their new companions, who were, in truth, very well worth looking at.

Four or five of them wore leopard-skin sashes across their bare, bony chests, to the no small interest of the boys, who recalled how Prince Jenor-Flan had told them that this was a proof of the wearer having slain the monster himself. Others had brass rings on their wrists and ankles, others still a huge bunch of rusty iron keys hung round the body by a cord of twisted palm-fibre. Most of them wore sugar-loaf caps of goat-skin very much like Robinson Crusoe's famous " topper," and not a few had their bodies hung (one could not say clothed) with red handkerchiefs and strips of blue or scarlet flannel, while the lower limbs were left quite uncovered, the effect being precisely that of an undersized ostrich.

But, lean and scraggy as they looked, these scarecrows had a show of muscle and sinew on their gaunt limbs which fully accounted for the surprising vigour that they displayed in driving their canoe through the water, and made Dick mentally decide that he would much rather shake hands with such men than fight them. The two lads, however, kept their thoughts to themselves, and said not a word; for Dr Strong had privately warned them, before starting, that whatever they did, they must keep up their dignity in the eyes of the savages, and that, if they began to talk, it would spoil all.

And now they were close to the line of gnashing, roaring breakers—and now they were right in the midst of them, and they were flung up and flung down, and pitched to and fro, and scourged with lashing spray till their eyes smarted; and ever and anon they would see a great hill of water hanging right overhead as if to bury them, and then they would find themselves safe over it, they could not tell how. Then, all in a moment, the uproar ceased as if by magic, the foam and fury were gone, and they were gliding calmly over the smooth, brown, oily waters of a small river, between two dark walls of matted boughs.

CHAPTER X

TO LIVE OR DIE ?

AND now, in one instant, the gloomy horror of the most dismal place on earth —the mouth of an African river—fell around them like a pall. Look which way they would, nothing was to be seen but the black, shadowy masses of the leathery mangroves, thrusting themselves out over the thick, foul, slimy water, and through the dark leaves that coiled round each other like writhing snakes, the rank white fever mist crept sullenly upward, like a breath of pestilence sent forth from the jaws of Death himself. Ever and anon, the swirl of the eddies in the wake of their boat left bare a broad, flat mud-bank, into the black, glistening surface of which the gaunt white mangrove roots

dug themselves hungrily, as if sucking
their vampire nourishment from the fathomless depths of slimy rottenness below.

But more gloomy by far than all the
outward hideousness of this evil place was
its sinister, tomb-like silence. No sight,
no sound of life broke the horrible and
unnatural repose of that ghastly maze of
distorted vegetation, which fully realized
the awful "living forest" seen by Dante
in the regions of the dead, every tree of
which was an agonized human form, writhing in torture as the merciless beaks of
the harpies tore its sentient boughs. The
desolation of untamed abundance—worse
a thousandfold than that desolation of
barrenness which one sees in the depths
of the Sahara and of the great Asiatic
deserts—was around them in all its terrors.

Nor did this valley of the shadow of
death lack an inhabitant—one in every
way worthy of it. At the splash of the
paddles, an answering ripple broke the

lifeless smoothness of the black, oily surface, and up through the sullen waters started, with a hoarse bellowing snort, the horny snout, small, cruel eye, and broad, scaly, mud-plastered back of a huge crocodile.

The two lads were not a little startled by the sudden springing up of this hideous brute almost within arm's length of them, and Eric, drawing hastily back, came within a hair's-breadth of falling right overboard. But not so the Malojas, who, so far from being startled or scared by this ghastly apparition, greeted the monster's coming with a burst of gleeful shouts and boyish laughter that awoke every echo oı the silent forests, seeming as much pleased as children at the appearance of a new game.

At once every hand clutched a weapon. The nearest man made a thrust with his long spear at the monster's narrow, cunning eye. A second man hit at the flat, scaly head with his paddle in passing ; and then came a puff of smoke and a loud bang from the bow of the boat, instantly followed by the report of a second gun from the other canoe.

The balls probably did not hit the crocodile at all, nor would they have hurt him much if they had, for the native guns of the West African coast are on a par with the " trade-musket " in the old story, which was warranted to kill three men at a shot—the man that fired it and the two who stood to right and left of him. But the river pirate seemed to think the odds against him too great, and vanished with a sullen grunt into the slimy depths below, giving a farewell lash of his monstrous tail that scourged the water into foam for many a yard around.

As he plunged, the savages sent after him a volley of choice native abuse, and one burly fellow (evidently the wag of the party), showing all his splendid white teeth in a boyish grin, uttered what was plainly held to be a first-rate joke by his comrades, for the roar of laughter that followed it shook the whole canoe from stem to stern.

But the general merriment suddenly died away into a grim and gloomy silence ; the laughing faces of the wild crew took all at once a grave and almost terrified air. The boys, looking up in surprise to see what all this meant, noticed that they had just come round a sharp bend of the river, and that right ahead of them jutted out into the stream a long, flat, sandy point, on which the riven trunk of a huge tree, white and blasted and dead, stood gauntly out against the dark background of shadowy thickets.

The travelled Dr Strong was at once reminded of an exactly similar spot that he had seen elsewhere—Demon Point on the Lower Gambia, of which he had told many a weird tale to his boy comrades, and their faces showed him that the

tomb, and the destroying there of all the articles that he used when in life, will send the ghosts of the slaves to serve their master with pipe and cup in the world of spirits as in that of men.

" Poor wretches ! " muttered Strong under his breath, " I hope we Christians will be able to teach them something better than that one of these days."

Even that dismal haunt of death, however, was not wholly unredeemed. Over these miserable wrecks of mortality the graceful syringa had twined lovingly its bright and tender blossoms, combating with its rich fragrance the foul reek of corruption—a mute but eloquent parable of how, amid the worst decay and degradation of man, spring up inexhaustibly the love and mercy of God.

And now a quick turn of the paddles sent the boat flying away to the right, at a rate that showed how eager the Malojas were to get clear of the dreaded spot.

They glided beneath a curtain of over-hanging boughs—which, amid the cheer-less gloom that filled this world of shadows, looked weirdly like skeleton hands extended to clutch them—and in a moment more they were speeding up a smaller river, which at this point ran into the gloomy stream that they had been traversing.

The new river, though small, ran swift and strong, and against its current they made but slow progress. The thinning trees showed them that the sun was already high in the sky, and our lads began to wonder how long they had been on the way and how much longer they were going to be.

It seemed, in fact, as if there were a good deal of the journey yet to come, for in another hour the savages made a halt, but instead of running alongside the bank, they moored their canoes to a rock in mid-stream, as far from either side as possible—an ominous precaution against wild beasts and snakes, and perhaps against hostile tribesmen likewise.

Here the Malojas took a light meal of fruit and cassava-bread, made from the pounded manioc root, and of this they gave a plentiful share to the English, who were treated, in fact, more as guests than as prisoners. Seeing this, the boys quite regained their wonted spirits, taking it for granted that this captivity among savages would be no such terrible affair after all, and would end in the approved story-book fashion, by their being ransomed and set free ; and Strong, if less confident (for it was the king, not this friendly escort, by whom their fate was to be decided), felt much more hopeful than before.

Two hours later they started again, and now their surroundings began to change visibly for the better. The foul fever-swamps were gone, the jungle was thinning fast, the banks were growing higher and firmer, and at last they came upon the first token of life and man's presence that they had yet seen in this great fortress of untamed nature—a cleared space along the right bank, on which the fan-like manioc and the vast green flags of the banana palm were set in orderly rows.

At this sign of their being near home, the paddlers quickened their stroke joyfully, and passing several other plantations of the same kind, shot away up a narrow creek and brought their boats to land, or rather to that custard of mingled land and water that passed for it in this spongy region, through which the whites were carried ashore, baby fashion, in the sturdy arms of the savages, who sank knee-deep at every step.

And now troubles began in earnest. The recent rains had turned into a flowing stream the thread-like path that led to the town, and they were forced to pick their way alternately along the right or left side of it—each in turn seeming worse than the other—till Dick was reminded of the Yankee boy in the old story : " Brother Tom's awfully mean to take the middle of the bed, and make me sleep on both sides of him ! " Moreover, at every step they ran an imminent risk of being scalped or impaled by projecting twigs or spiky bosses of prickly pear ; and at every ten paces or so came a vast puddle, in leaping over (or into) which, they splashed each other so thoroughly as to look like strips of blotting-paper running a race across an ink-stand.

But, by dint of skipping when they could and wading when they could not, they at last got safe to the " town," such as it was.

Evidently the " white faces " were still a novelty in this wild region, for at the first glimpse of the travellers, men, women and children came flocking from every side and pressed round them with shrill cries of amazement, and the boys, while thus stared at, found plenty to stare at in turn.

The town was protected by a high palisade of sharp stakes, bound together with stout withes. Most of the houses were queer little birds' nests of wicker-work smeared with mud and roofed with dried palm-leaves, and not a few consisted merely of a thick grass thatch supported on four strong stakes, the whole effect being very much that of a door-mat hung out to dry on the points of four walking sticks.

On the right, as they passed along, they saw a huge hollowed log, with a curiously-shaped opening cut in its flattened top ; and the lads knew it at once for one of the great war-drums of which Dick's father had said so much in his letters. On the left a strapping negress (with the blue stripe, denoting free birth, where her fore-head ought to have been had she had any) was pounding in a wooden trough a quantity of manioc roots—the acid smell of which

L

half-choked the boys in passing—while her baby, a funny little monkey, with nothing on but a brass neck-ring, gazed wonder-ingly at the "white chiefs" as they went by.

Next they saw an earthen plate nailed on a dead palm-tree as a kind of "ju-ju" (magic charm) and through the open door-way of a hut they espied a battered leather portmanteau of English make, marked with the initials "T. L. P.," evidently the spoil of some wreck. On the wall of another hut was fixed a brightly painted tablet (plainly an object of great reverence to the natives) bearing in gilt letters the inscription "Tonic Vermifuge."

Into this latter hut (which was rather larger than the rest, and seemed to belong to some man of note) the tall chief, Karri, led the four castaways, who were no sooner in than they heard the door made fast behind them.

"Here we are, then," said Strong, "and

here we must stay till the king is ready for us; and I hope he won't be long!" added he in the tone of one thinking aloud rather than speaking to his comrades.

He had voiced their thoughts as well as his own, for, with John Bull's natural inclination to meet a peril half-way, they were eager to end the intolerable suspense by getting it all over at once.

The boys looked anxiously through the small square opening that served as a window, which commanded a full view of the town and the river beyond it, but nothing was to be seen of the king, and they were just drawing back disappointed, when from the far distance came, thrice repeated, the deep, hollow boom of a war-drum.

"Aha!" cried Strong, "that's the signal that the king is coming; he must have been away somewhere."

Boom! boom! boom! replied the great war-drum of the town from its place; and then came a deafening clamour of shouting, horn-blowing, and beating of brass pans, which grew ten-fold louder as a large canoe, curiously carved and ornamented, was seen gliding down the dark river, propelled by twelve sturdy negroes with leopard-skin sashes across their bare chests and small brass plates on their woolly hair, evidently the badge of the king's body-guard.

The whole stern of the canoe was hid by an enormous umbrella (always the sign of royalty in West Africa) almost as big as a small cricket tent, with an embroidered fringe several inches long. Each division of it was of a different colour—red, green, yellow, blue, purple, or white—and bore the figure of some animal, the scarlet section a lion, the blue one a crocodile, the white one a snake, and so on.

The umbrella came ashore, seemingly all by itself—for nothing was to be seen of any one underneath it—and then began a

din to which all that had gone before was
nothing, the horn-blowing and pan-beating
being supplemented with a ceaseless boom-
ing of the great war-drum and the firing
off of muskets by the score.

Then came a sudden hush in the uproar.
A few minutes later the door of the hut
opened and before them stood, with six of
the king's guards at his back, the tall,
gaunt form of Karri, who, with a look of
unwonted excitement, signed to them to
follow him.

There was no choice but to obey, and
forth they went to the presence of the man
who was to decide whether they were to
live or die !

CHAPTER XI

DOOMED

THROUGH a town that had suddenly grown silent the four captives were led up to the king's judgment-seat. They walked between two walls of eager faces and jostling shoulders, but the clamorous crowd was awed into stillness by a crisis which, to the white strangers, meant the issue of life or death.

In the centre of the town stood, all by itself (as if the meaner houses had drawn back from it in reverence), a hut of unusual size, painted in staring colours and adorned with various quaint carvings. Just in front of it was one of the open pole-and-thatch shelters, in which, with his armed guards ranged on either side, sat under the shade of the royal umbrella the Maloja king himself.

But at their approach the umbrella was slightly raised, and as they caught sight of the face which it had hidden till then, even the cool doctor started as if he were shot, and Dick, springing forward, seized the king by both hands, and shouted at the top of his voice :

" Jenor-Flan, and no mistake ! "

At the same moment Eric, with a hurrah worthy of the best hit in a cricket match, whipped the shell chain off his own neck and put it round that of its rightful owner.

The gazing throng watched this strange scene with eyes starting out of their heads, and their amazement was redoubled as they saw the king rise from his place and return the strangers' friendly greetings with the heartiest goodwill. Then he said a few words to the crowd in his own tongue, which were answered with a shout that seemed to shake the very earth.

" Me tell dem all you my frien' ! " explained King Jenor-Flan in broken

Portuguese ; " now you hab good hut, hab all you want. Little while, you come chop (eat) wid me, den we hab big palaver (talk)."

Hardly had they left the royal presence when the tide of popular enthusiasm burst upon " the king's friends " in earnest. They were borne back to their hut shoulder-high by a shouting crowd, Kabembi following with a smile of quiet amusement, and when, an hour later, they found themselves dining with the ex-slave of Madeira in the character of King of the Malojas, with all the people outside cheering, drumming, and firing off guns in their honour, the boys could hardly believe that they were not in a dream.

But even this astounding change from prisoners to royal favourites could not make Dick Fernott forget for a moment his father's peril, and he took the first chance of telling the young king all about the Colonel's capture, and his present dangerous situation.

"JENOR-FLAN, AND NO MISTAKE!"

Jenor-Flan started visibly at the news that this kidnapped Englishman, of whom he had already heard so much, was his former friend's own father, and he at once sent off one of his best men to scout through the Mbantu country (with the language of which the man was familiar) and to find out how matters stood with " the good white man."

" You no fear—me help you ! " said he heartily ; and all three felt much comforted.

Meanwhile Kabembi, the Jaloofa, was having a fine time of it on his own account. As an attendant of the great white chiefs who were such friends of the king himself, he had a full share of their glory, and, after being feasted to his heart's content, he related to an admiring audience, through the medium of a man who knew something of the Jaloofa tongue, the whole story of his adventures with the white men.

On the following morning, the travellers paid the king a second visit, and he then explained, in reply to the boys' eager questions, the mystery of his strange disappearance a year before.

His father's death in war had left him heir to the throne; but his ambitious uncle, who had long since marked it for his own, had betrayed the lad into the hands of a slave-hunting gang, who carried him off to Madeira with other prisoners and sold him to Dom Pablo da Silva.

For a time his people thought him dead, but the chief Karri, one of his staunchest adherents, at length learned by chance what had become of him, and (the usurper having fallen in battle just at that time) stirred up the whole tribe to attempt his rescue. Several of his men who had served as seamen on British or Spanish ships sailed for Madeira in quest of him in a hired vessel—her owner, a Portuguese half-breed, acting as captain—and succeeded in effecting his escape.

" Fader chain," he ended, laying his

hand on the precious necklace, " me plenty glad get him 'gain ! "

The very next day, back came their scout from the Mbantu country with evil tidings. The Mbantus had been goaded to fury by Colonel Fernott's steadfast refusal to alter his decision and make over the disputed land to them ; and the native priests had declared that a human sacrifice was needed to appease the wrath of their gods, and that this insolent stranger was the very man for the purpose. The suggestion had found favour in the eyes of the tribe, and, on the third day from that time, at sunrise, the Colonel was to be put to death as a victim, with all the horrors of African cruelty.

Poor Dick all but went out of his mind at the fearful news, and Eric was quite as bad. Even Dr Strong himself fairly lost, for once, the coolness for which he was famous.

Their first idea was to appeal to Kabembi

who, knowing the Mbantus as he did, and
being their declared enemy, might be able
to give good counsel as to the best way
of attacking them and rescuing the Colonel.
But the Jaloofa was nowhere to be found,
and they now called to mind that none of
them had seen him since the day before.

Had he deserted to the enemy, and
betrayed their plans ? Surely it could not
be !

But Jenor-Flan, when they told him of
this, only said with a knowing smile :

" Me know where him gone, you see
him 'gain soon."

With a vigour and promptitude beyond
his years, the young king had already sent
off runners to call out all his men for a
raid into the Mbantu country. The mere
mention of such a thing was enough for
these born fighters, who came trooping
down in hundreds, and ere nightfall the
whole town, and all the country round
it, swarmed with a muster of sturdy

Jenor-Flan, he conferred with him apart for a few moments.

Then the young king's face grew as bright as his own, and presently a sturdy black was seen to shoulder the box, carry it down to the landing-place, and stow it carefully in the bow of the king's own canoe.

The first stroke of the paddles made Dick's heart leap, as he felt that at last they were fairly on the way to rescue his father, with a force that seemed well able to do it, judging by the strength of the men, and the great number of them who were armed with guns. But his heart sank again as Jenor-Flan, when the boy hinted as much to him, replied with a very grave look :

" We need all dem gun, for sure ; Mbantu got plenty gun, too."

In ascending the river to reach the Mbantu country, they had to pass through that of the Jaloofas ; and here a new surprise awaited them. As they passed, at noon on the day after leaving Jenor-Flan's town, the mouth of a small stream that marked the frontier of the Jaloofa territory, they were greeted with a burst of welcoming shouts, and a second fleet of war canoes came out to join them, manned by the best warriors of the Jaloofa tribe, foremost among whom was the missing Kabembi himself !

In fact, the ex-slave of Fernando Po had proved to be a priceless ally.

When he brought word to his people that the Malojas were on the way to fall upon the hated Mbantus, the whole tribe, as he had foreseen, was at once on fire to join in the attack, and to settle, once for all, the pending dispute over the contested land. A swift runner was sent off to tell Jenor-Flan when and where to expect them, and here they were in full force, as eager for action as the young king himself.

The boys grew radiant at sight of this

important accession of strength, which fully doubled their force at one stroke; and now they deemed Dick's father to be as good as saved already, for, from all that they had heard, it seemed impossible for the Mbantus, drained as their strength had been by recent wars, to make head against this combined attack.

Poor lads! they little knew what was to come.

That day all went well, and by the next morning the united fleets were so far up the river that, to all appearance, nightfall would find them within easy reach of the Mbantus' border town, where Colonel Fernott was in prison, and where he was to be sacrificed on the following day. Once there, their success was all but certain, and all alike were joyful and triumphant, as men so often are on the very eve of some great and crushing calamity.

The keen-eyed Kabembi, who knew this

M

part of the river well, was the first to notice that its waters seemed to be strangely low for the time of year ; but he said nothing of it to his comrades, wishing to be quite sure of the fact ere he called their attention to it.

But ere long it became so manifest that all the rest could see it as plainly as himself, and the farther they went up the stream, the more glaringly evident it was. Rocks that usually lay right under the water were now several feet above it, and there was so little water on some of the shoals with which that part of the river abounded, that one or two of the larger canoes actually scraped the sand in getting over them !

What could this mean ? It was now the height of the rainy season, when all the river-beds ought to have been full to overflowing ; yet this stream was lower than they had ever seen it before !

A strange, haunting disquiet began to creep over the eager lads, who became

more and more uneasy as they noticed
the grave and anxious looks of all around
them. Even the young king's bright face
was clouded, and Karri's wore a look of
deepening gloom, very rare indeed on those
bold, manly features.

At length, just as the sun had set, they
came to the point where their course made
a sudden bend to the left, following a
wide curve of the river, which would bring
them up to the other side of the Mbantu
town, the side on which no attack could
be expected. They would thus take the
enemy quite by surprise, and (so Kabembi
had told them) barely two hours would
suffice to carry them thither, whereas they
had fully twelve to spare before the fatal
sunrise that was to give the signal of
death !

Success was sure, then ; onward to victory !

" It's a good job for us, though, that
we were able to come by boat," whispered
Dick to Eric, " for just look at that swamp

CHAPTER XII

THE LAST SUNRISE

In a large hut in the centre of the Mbantu town lay, bound hand and foot, the doomed Colonel Fernott, counting the few remaining hours which were all that was left to him of life. At sunrise he was to die—to die a cruel and shameful death, with no friend near him and none but the scowling eyes of mortal foes to watch his last agonies.

He had no hope of escape, no hope of release. He was firmly bound and securely guarded; even had he been free, he could not have told in what direction lay the nearest friendly district, and he knew better than to hope for any mercy from the ferocious enemies to whom its very name was unknown. There was nothing left for him now but to die as a Christian man should do.

It seemed hard to perish thus by the

hands of brutal savages, far from home and friends, just as a prospect of long years of quiet in England, and home comforts, and the peace and happiness of which he had dreamed so long had opened upon him at last. But the man whose name his brother officers had justly turned into "Fear-nought" was not one to lament over the inevitable, or to whine for pity when no pity was to be hoped for, and he faced his doom as manfully as he had faced all the other perils and sufferings of his stormy life.

Would Dick ever know how his father had died ? and how would he bear the news ? If he could but have seen the boy just once more—but what was the use of thinking of that now ?

Slowly and wearily the leaden hours crept by, and now the fatal sunrise could not be far away, which was to be the last that he would ever see. The brave man commended his soul to God, and rallied all his firmness to meet his impending doom.

the two lads heartily echoed the fervent "Thank God!" uttered by Dr Strong when the good news was translated to him.

Then the king turned to Kabembi, and, pointing to the heavy gold bracelets on his own bare arms, said with great emphasis :

"Make good your words, Jaloofa friend, and these shall be yours, and others as well."

"There needs no reward, O King," said the other proudly ; "the white chiefs have been good to me."

So saying, he leaped from his boat on to a grass tussock that seemed hardly equal to the sustaining of his weight—bent forward and peered into the undergrowth—then went down on hands and knees, and, parting the wild grass, looked keenly to right and left for a moment—and then he called out that the path was found, and stepped fearlessly into the hideous labyrinth.

"For your lives, follow me close, and tread just where I do!" said he as he did so.

And in a short time the whole host were winding through that gloomy maze in single file, each stepping warily in the footprints of the man before him.

Just at first the great bell-like flowers and delicate ferns that fringed the edge of the morass, fed by its overflowing moisture, almost belied the grim reputation of this evil place. But as they began to go deeper and deeper into the forest of giant reeds and long rank grass that rose far above their heads, its depressing influence stole over them with a slow, creeping horror that even their iron nerves could not resist. The cool and hardy doctor himself, in the midst of all these stout comrades, was oppressed with a haunting sense of fearful isolation, as he felt that one false step might doom him at any moment to a certain and hideous death in the depths of that ghastly quagmire, from which the hundreds of brave men before and behind him—some of whom were all painted on the side, they understood it all in a moment.

Forth stepped Dr Strong to carry out his own plan, and Kabembi, who had seen signal-rockets used on ship-board, acted as his assistant. Up flew the first rocket with a whiz and a roar, and down it came on the grass roofs in a shower of sparks, followed by a howl of terror from Fernott's guards, who took to their heels at once, yelling as they ran.

The Mbantus, alarmed by the uproar, swarmed out in hundreds, only to find their town in flames; for the first rocket had kindled several of the dry grass-thatches, and the second (which went off just then) fired half a dozen more. The fire ran like lightning from hut to hut, and in a few moments the whole place was one red and roaring blaze.

To the bewildered and terrified savages (who had never seen anything of the kind before) it seemed as if their town was being destroyed by fire from heaven, for no enemy was to be seen. The Mbantus, one and all, fled like sheep, without looking behind them; and ere the last man had disappeared, Dr Strong and Jenor-Flan had burst open the door of Colonel Fernott's prison, and set him free.

The Colonel's voyage down the river, through the country of the grateful Jaloofas (who had not forgotten that it was in their cause that he had perilled his life), was one continued triumph. It may be that these born warriors were a little disappointed with a victory that had been achieved without the firing of a shot, or the slaying of a single enemy—a fact for which Dr Strong, on his part, was deeply thankful. But they were amply consoled by getting possession of the long-disputed land once for all, for the Mbantus had been so thoroughly scared that they never ventured near the fatal place again.

Jenor-Flan himself, and a picked body of

his best men, escorted the English party down to the nearest port, where they could get a steamer for England; and when they took leave of him (with what heartfelt gratitude may be imagined), he said earnestly to Colonel Fernott, in his own language, which the latter well understood:

"When you get back to your own land, Chief of the English, send me some of those good white teachers who show men how to be wise, and to love each other, and to pray to the Great Father who lives up in the sky, and as they say, so will I and my people do."

The young king kept his word. The missionaries, when they came, received a hearty welcome, and when, in after years, Dick and Eric visited their former friend once more, they found him reigning as a Christian king over a Christian people.